The Threader

By Solovey

101 Panya Publishing

Cover Art by ChatGPT

ISBN-13: 978-1-988880-09-9

ISBN-10: 1-988880-09-2

BISAC: FIC040000 FICTION / Jewish

Table of Contents

Prologue

This story will brush against your heart like the whisper of silk, tender and fleeting, then linger like a wound. It fades, yes, but never truly vanishes. A scar remains: a quiet echo of pain etched into permanence.

Life is often called a journey. But picture it instead as a train—gliding through mist and memory, pausing at places, both familiar and strange. You step off for a while: into love, into loss, into stillness. And then you move on. The engine's heartbeat aligns with your own, steady and unrelenting, carrying you forward to where fate waits, silent and unseen.

As you go, you carry more than just your belongings. You carry your scars—silent testaments to what you've endured. You carry joy—bright blossoms in the light of spring. You carry memory—layered and living. And above all, you carry your bloodline—an invisible thread spun through time, weaving you to those who came before, will appear after, and those who wait beyond.

You are not alone on this journey. You are the story. You are the thread. You are.

Chapter One
Heart

Ana pulled back the heavy burgundy drapes. Central Park stretched before her—framed like a living tapestry in early autumn. The trees blazed with reds and golds—nature's quiet reminder that life moves on, even after the longest winters.

She stood still, letting the city breathe into her: the low hum of taxis, the faint sirens in the distance, the first crisp bite of fall in the air. Below, the streets buzzed with life. But up here, in her Fifth Avenue apartment, time felt suspended. She moved to the kitchen and poured herself a cup of tea. The kettle whistled gently, the steam curling like a memory.

Ana was in her seventies now. Her silver-streaked hair was short and neatly styled, and her posture was upright but softened with age. The lines on her face were gentle, carved by years of laughter, grief, and everything in between. Her sharp, steady, kind blue eyes swept over the quiet apartment.

The space was light-filled and calm, decorated with intention and restraint. Her silk scarves hung like preserved moments on the walls—each embroidered with roses, no two alike. Framed in black wood, they seemed to float, petals frozen in motion.

One scarf hung alone, just slightly apart from the rest—the first. A deep crimson rose on ash-gray silk. It was for Roza—her daughter. Her lost girl. The girl with the scar. And Ana's own scar, too—the kind that never fully closes.

In the corner, Abraham, or as Ana called him, Abi, a boy about eight, sat curled into the weathered armchair, a book in his lap. He was small and pale, almost translucent in the morning light. His dark eyes flicked up from the page as she entered.

"Did you sleep all right?" Ana asked softly, wrapping her hands around the warm mug.

He nodded. "I dreamed of snow. But it wasn't cold."

She smiled. "Then it must've been Russian snow."

He considered that. "Do you think she used to dream about snow too?"

Ana didn't answer right away. Her fingers tightened slightly around the cup.

A year ago, Abi's failing heart had been replaced with one from a girl halfway across the world—a girl who had died too young. A girl with no voice left, but a gift that beat steadily in his chest.

"I hope she dreamed about good things," Ana said finally. "Snow, maybe. Or sunflowers."

"Why sunflowers?" Abi asked.

"Because they turn their faces to the light," she said. "Even when it hurts."

He looked back down at the book but didn't turn the page. Ana watched him for a moment, her chest tightening with a swell of love so fierce it almost hurt. This boy—this fragile miracle—was the thread connecting her past to whatever future still remained. The heart inside him wasn't just a medical wonder. It was a living reminder that even after unimaginable loss, something still grew.

She crossed the room and touched his shoulder gently.

"You know they're coming today," she said. Abi nodded again. "The girl's family."

"The ones who lost what we almost did."

He didn't speak, but his lip trembled just slightly.

Ana knelt beside him. "It's okay to be nervous."

"I'm not nervous," he said, but he didn't meet her eyes. "But Doctor Vera will be there."

She smiled, brushing his hair back from his forehead.

"Vera will be there," she said.

Abi gave a tiny nod. "Bepa means belief," he whispered.

"Yes," she said. "And sometimes, belief is all we have left."

He looked at her, eyes darker than before but clear.

That made him look up. "Really?"

"Absolutely," she whispered. "But some things… Some things are too important to avoid. Even when they hurt."

A distant honk cut through the quiet like a school bell, not meant for them but somehow still ringing in their bones. It was a signal. It was time.

Ana took a deep breath and looked once more at the framed scarf on the wall. It held a history locked and stretched. Today, the past and the present would meet, and maybe—just maybe—some broken pieces could begin to come back together.

She didn't know what she would say. Some things had no words. But still, she would try.

Chapter Two
Before

Ana was born in a house that smelled of starch and thread. Her earliest memories held the soft rhythm of scissors gliding through cloth, the gentle snap of fabric folding under skilled hands, and the dry snap of a ruler on the cutting table. Her mother's voice wove through the room—a delicate tapestry of murmured prayers in Yiddish and soft lullabies sung in Ukrainian, blending ancient comfort with tender love. The melodies rose and fell like a quiet breeze, wrapping Ana in warmth even before she understood the words, embedding in her a sense of home stitched from both faith and homeland.

Their home was small—two rooms above her father's tailor shop in a Ukrainian town no one ever wrote about—but it was orderly, clean, and always filled with the abundance of never-ending work.

Her father, Yitzhak Nityak, or the threader, was a tailor like his father, his grandfather, and many before him. He was tall, bony, and precise, with thick glasses and an air of quiet endurance. He spoke little, but his silences spoke volumes—measured disapproval, quiet principles, an old-world discipline carried in his posture like a spine made of iron thread. He believed in boundaries: between work and rest, between outsiders and their own, between tradition and risk.

Her mother, Miriam, was smaller, rounder, and full of soft singing and sharp opinions. She cooked while mending sleeves, corrected Ana's Hebrew as she threaded needles, and scolded gently—often with a kiss afterward. She believed in customs—not because they were beautiful, but because they were necessary. They had kept the family together through years of uncertainty. They were the rules that made life bearable in a place that could turn on you without warning.

They had built their world carefully, stitch by stitch, word by word, year by year.

Ana was their only child. A late child. A miracle child, her mother said. After years of an empty house, she came screaming into the world just as the snow melted in the spring of 1924. Her mother cried when she was born—not from pain, but from the terror of finally holding something she feared would be taken away.

From a young age, Ana watched the world from behind bolts of cloth. She would hide under the sewing tables and listen—men coming to be measured for coats, women whispering secrets while fitting their daughters for wedding dresses. The shop was more than a place of business—it was the heart of the community, and Ana happily absorbed every bit of it.

But over time, the steady hum of the shop began to soften. Visitors grew scarce, their footsteps hesitant on the worn wooden floor. Warm smiles faded into cautious glances, and familiar faces became fleeting shadows. The air thickened with an unspoken tension, as if the town itself held its breath beneath a tightening veil. Whispered fears, quiet warnings, and invisible borders drawn in silence wove through the streets like a fragile thread—pulling taut, threatening to unravel all they had carefully stitched together.

And yet—the shop persisted, a fragile thread holding fast in a world unravelling. It was the only rhythm they knew, the sole certainty amid shrinking streets and wary glances of once-familiar faces. Life continued—soft, stubborn, and slow—stitch by stitch.

Ana kept sewing. It was the one thing she truly knew—she had learned to sew before she learned to write. By the time she was twelve, she could hem a skirt in under an hour. By fourteen, she designed embroidery patterns her mother proudly stitched into dresses and pillowcases. Her fingers were constantly moving—tying, pinning, threading, stitching roses onto the vyshyvankas worn by the maidens in town. There was something sacred in the act of making beauty from scraps, as if every thread was a quiet defiance against the ordinary.

Still, even in the warmth of home, Ana knew she was different. The world outside was shifting. Whispers about Jews, about new laws coming from far-off places—she heard them all. But inside their home and shop, the world was still soft, still safe.

It was Vasyl who pulled her outside of it.

He was not Jewish. He was not safe. He was not careful with his words or his laughter. He worked the fields with his brothers and came to town on Sundays, smelling of earth and sun. He brought her wildflowers and called her "his firebird." At first, she ignored him. Then she smiled. Then she couldn't stop thinking about him.

Her parents were furious: he was not one of them—not by blood, not by faith, not by heritage or name. He was a goy—a stranger who walked on different paths and spoke in different rhythms. Outsiders were welcomed, smiled at, fed, and nodded to—but never trusted.

He worked on Saturdays, crossed himself before meals, and did not understand the weight of a mezuzah on a doorframe or why Ana lit two candles on Friday nights, even when the world felt indifferent. He smiled too easily at things her father frowned upon, and he asked questions that her mother called dangerous.

When Ana told her parents she loved him, her mother cried—not out of cruelty, but out of fear. To them, he was an outsider crossing invisible lines—an intruder in a world stitched tightly by tradition and history.

"You think love will protect you?" Miriam had said, wringing her hands. "The world doesn't care who you love. It cares who you are."

Yitzhak didn't say a word. He just turned away, the silence cutting deeper than any argument.

But Ana had been raised in that silence and knew how to push through it. Her love for Vasyl wasn't rebellion—it was belief. That two people from different worlds could build a third, together. That home didn't have to look like the past to hold the future.

At seventeen, she married him anyway. She wore a simple dress with sleeves that she embroidered herself. No chuppah. No rabbi. Just the town clerk and Vasyl's hands, shaking as he slipped the ring on her finger.

They moved into a small hut near the woods, where the wind sounded like the sea and the stars felt closer. Ana made curtains. Vasyl built a crib. She taught him Hebrew songs. He taught her how to shoot a rifle and plant tomatoes.

She was happy. Not foolishly. Just… quietly.

In the spring, she found out she was pregnant. She painted tiny birds on the wall where they put the crib and sewed a baby blanket lined with rosebuds.

The baby kicked early, danced inside her. Ana already gave her the name. Roza.

Chapter Three
Hunger

Sometimes, when she stirred lentils in the pot or shaped dough with her palms, Ana remembered being hungry enough to cry without sound—not empty, not tired, but hollow—as if a silent scream had carved out her bones.

It happened when she was eight. She was still small enough to slip beneath the kitchen table and pretend it was a house of her own. But old enough to sense that the quiet happiness of their home was slipping away. Yitzhak stopped taking her to the market, which had been their quiet Sunday tradition—just the two of them, shopping for fresh vegetables. Miriam began stretching the food: there were no second helpings anymore, and she was always the last to fill her plate, half full.

Then the winter of 1932 came early. Snow fell before the leaves had finished turning. Her father, Yitzhak, had begun storing whatever grain he could trade in the attic, convinced that "this year, something is wrong." And he was right. People in town whispered of new restrictions, trucks rumbling away with sacks of grain, men taken for speaking out.

Then came the hunger. It wasn't a war—not yet—but it felt like one. First, the flour disappeared. Then the potatoes. Even the weeds stopped growing. Ana's mother boiled water with a few grains—no potatoes, no cabbage, no carrots—and pretended it was soup.

One neighbour's child died. Then another. Their eyes grew too large for their faces, their bellies swollen like sacks of potatoes—heavy, round, and strange—bulging with a hunger that twisted their bodies. The bellies were taut and misshapen, a cruel mimicry of nourishment, like the rough burlap sacks the grain trucks carried away—filled, yet hollow inside. Their voices turned high and strange, like birds trapped in cages, fluttering against ribs too weak to fly. Ana learned not to ask questions. Learned to eat slowly, to pretend her mouth was full even when it wasn't.

Her mother's hands grew raw from scrubbing—constantly scrubbing, even when there was nothing left to clean—as if she could wash the hunger out of the world.

Vasyl's silence sometimes settled heavy in the air, a quiet grief that never needed words. One evening, as Ana hummed a lullaby softly to the baby growing inside her, he spoke from the shadowed corner of the room.

"There was a brother once," he said quietly. "He never heard a lullaby."

Ana's voice faltered but kept going, the tune wrapping around her belly, around the small life stirring within her: "Spi, moya radist, spi…" ("Sleep, my joy, sleep…")

"I sing for you," she whispered, "for the one who came before, and the one who's coming now."

Vasyl stepped closer and gently placed his hand over hers: "I wonder if he would have liked your song."

Ana smiled softly: "Maybe he does now."

They sat together in the stillness, the past and the future entwined in the quiet melody.

They survived because her father had once sewn a greatcoat for a Soviet officer. Quietly, the officer's wife came to their door one cold morning, carrying a rough burlap sack. The sack was heavy and coarse against her hands, its faded threads straining under the weight of potatoes, their skins mottled and dusted with soil. She handed it over with a look that was both apology and sorrow, the faint scent of expensive perfume mingling oddly with the damp earth and the chill of winter.

That sack of potatoes lasted three months.

Ana never forgot her name-Vera—or the look in her eyes, the fine line of fur at her cuffs that seemed so out of place in their small, starving world.

Later, when people spoke of strength and endurance, Ana would nod and smile. But she remembered the potato soup, her mother's trembling hands, and the bellies swollen like those rough sacks—full of hunger but somehow still holding on.

Now, years later, standing barefoot in her small kitchen with a life growing inside her, Ana sang softly to the baby. Vasyl sat outside, carving wood. The radio murmured Soviet propaganda songs. The baby kicked.

Ana touched her belly and whispered, "Maybe you'll like my lullabies too."

And Ana, who had survived hunger and silence, closed her eyes and prayed, "Please let it stay like this. Just a little bit longer."

Chapter Four
Zhar-Ptitsa (Firebird)

Vasyl called her his Zhar-Ptitsa. He said it the first time he noticed her sitting by the window, singing and stitching as the sky turned lavender and her cheeks caught the last red light of day. The sun fell across her hair like flame, and for a moment she looked less like a girl and more like something uncatchable—fierce, bright, untamed.

"Zhar-Ptitsa," he said softly, almost to himself.

The name stayed, first in his mind, and when he got the courage to approach her, it became her nickname. Firebird—wild, glowing, not meant to be caged.

He would find excuses to pass by the window again, carrying nothing in particular. She would hum a little louder when she saw him approach.

Once, he dropped a folded note near the bench she always used. It had only two words: "Still singing?" She didn't answer right away. The next day, she wore a red ribbon in her braid.

They spoke slowly when they finally did—halting words, more smiles than sentences. Their hands never quite touched that first season. But the warmth between them lingered like spring trying to thaw a long winter.

They were happy, yes. But not simple.

The hut they shared had barely two rooms: a narrow entryway and one room for everything else—life, eating, sleep. It stood on the forest's edge, far from her town and his village.

"Neutral ground," Vasyl joked.

But Ana knew it was exile—quiet and chosen, but exile all the same.

At night, she still whispered the Shema before sleep. Quietly. Under her breath.

Vasyl lit candles the Orthodox way, crossed himself at cemeteries, and refused to eat meat during Lent. He didn't stop her from keeping her own rituals. But he didn't understand them either.

And sometimes… that mattered.

One Friday morning, she was shaping dough into round loaves for Shabbat—or Friday dinner, as she explained it—when he walked in and asked, offhand,

"Why always round? What's the point?"

She flinched.

It wasn't the question. It was the tone. Like something sacred could be reduced to a shape. Like centuries of tradition could be brushed aside with a shrug.

She didn't answer. Just kept kneading, her hands white with flour.

Later, he came behind her and gently touched the small part of her back.

"I didn't mean it like that," he said. "It's just… we do things differently, that's all."

She nodded. But her heart had already folded in on itself, just a little—a small, papery crease.

The truth was, her parents had begged her not to marry him. Not because they didn't believe in love—they did. But because they had lived long enough to know what the world did to people like Ana and Vasyl. People who didn't fit into boxes. People who built homes on the borderlines.

Her mother refused to come to the wedding. Her father came, but didn't speak. Still, Ana chose Vasyl. Again and again.

When the bread rose.

When his boots tracked mud across her clean floor.

When he laughed so loudly, the trees shook.

When he whispered to her belly at night, singing folk songs from his childhood to the baby that was coming.

And he chose her—when the villagers muttered, when his own brother stopped speaking to him, when he was offered a better house if he left "the Jewess."

They chose each other, even when the world didn't.

On Friday nights, when Ana lit two small candles and whispered blessings her mother had taught her, she sometimes felt her family's silence pressing in. She missed her father's tallis by the door, the smell of her mother's stew, and being understood without needing to explain.

And Vasyl, who believed love could overcome anything, stood in the doorway watching her—helpless to reach the origins of where she had come from.

That winter, they made curtains together. She sewed; he hammered nails.

Outside, the rumours grew louder. Neighbours talked about Hitler, about new borders, and about things that couldn't be spoken aloud. But inside their small house, there was still bread on the table and warmth under the covers.

And Ana, belly round with life, would sometimes lie awake and think: I don't know what will happen. But I know love like this deserves to be."

Chapter Five
Roza

Roza was born just before the sirens and cannonades.

The windows were still shut against the chill, and outside, the trees stood in stiff, silent salute. Ana gave one long, low cry, and the world stilled—quiet enough to hear the girl's first breath.

She was small. Not weak, just delicate, like something finely made. A bundle of warmth wrapped in an old towel, dark curls damp on her head. Her nose—not sharp like Ana's father's, not broad like Vasyl's. Something entirely her own.

Vasyl had run to fetch the midwife, but Roza hadn't waited for permission. She arrived with stubbornness already in her lungs.

When he came back, panting, his boots tracking dirt across the kitchen floor, Ana looked up from the bundle in her arms.

"She's here," she said, voice hoarse with disbelief.

"She's perfect," he whispered.

And she was. Perfect.

For a few weeks, they lived in that fragile kind of happiness—the kind you don't trust, but dare to hold anyway. Ana stayed in bed with Roza curled on her chest. She whispered lullabies her mother used to sing in Yiddish, soft and steady like prayers. Vasyl came home each night with bread, potatoes, and news from the village—who was hiding what, who had already gone, who had been taken.

But the walls of their tiny home still held. For now. For a moment.

They named her Roza—like the flower and like Ana's grandmother in Krakow, who had died after the pogroms with nothing but a prayer on her lips—a name soaked in memory, sorrow, and the kind of beauty that survives.

For Ana, Roza was the answer to a prayer she hadn't dared to say aloud. She imagined a hundred futures for her little girl.

Roza at five, running barefoot through the garden with wild braids and mud on her skirt.

Roza at nine, asking too many questions at once, daring the boys to outclimb her.

Roza at twelve, reading poetry with her head tilted, as if it were a sacred text.

At thirteen, her Bat Mitzvah—a rite of strength, of belonging.

At sixteen, falling in love—maybe with a kind Jewish boy, maybe not. Someone who would understand the weight she carried in her blood.

Roza, as an old woman, someday, her forehead still marked by the faint scar from the fall, and Ana, even older and frail, telling her, "That mark? That's how I knew you were mine."

A future imagined, lit by the dim flame of hope.

But one thing did happen. Roza was three months old. Ana had laid her on the bed to sleep, just for a second while she stirred the barley.

One thump. One cry. The baby had rolled off the edge and hit her head on the wooden floor. Blood. Screaming. Ana wrapped her in a shawl and ran barefoot through the frost to the midwife. She didn't feel the ice biting her feet until much later.

The wound healed. But the scar remained—a pale, narrow line across Roza's smooth little forehead. Ana couldn't stop staring at it. Not just with guilt. But with fear. As if the world had signed its name too early on her child's skin.

"She'll be fierce," Vasyl said, brushing Roza's hair aside.

"She'll be marked," Ana whispered.

The scar became a secret promise—a line between what was, and what would never be.

Then came the arguments—small, sharp, sudden.

Vasyl's mother brought a priest. Ana stared at him, eyes hard.

"She needs protection," Halyna said, matter—of—fact.

"She has me," Ana answered.

"But she lives here. Among us."

"She is mine."

"She is also ours."

They baptized her anyway. Behind Ana's back. A bowl of water in a neighbour's shed. Ana found out weeks later. She didn't scream. She didn't speak. She simply lit two candles that Friday night and rocked Roza in the dark, singing a lullaby to her daughter.

And yet-Ana loved them. All of them. Even Vasyl's mother, Halyna, in her own way. The war would soon take many things, but it hadn't yet stolen tenderness.

Ana still traced Roza's cheeks with the back of her hand, whispering names of ancestors like prayers. She still stitched a tiny Star of David into the hem of her baby's blanket, invisible to anyone but her. She still believed that if she held them tightly enough-Roza, Vasyl, the candlelight—the world might hold off a while longer.

It didn't.

But that moment—that sliver of peace, of a new life, of Roza cradled between two worlds—that was real. It lived inside Ana like a heartbeat.

And even years later, in another country, another life, when the sky over New York looked nothing like the sky over Ukraine, Ana would close her eyes and remember the weight of her baby girl—soft and fierce, a scar blooming too early on her forehead—and wonder, what if?

What if the world had given her time? What if that small life had been allowed to unfold—like a thread not knotted, not cut too soon? Sometimes Ana thought she could still feel that invisible thread tugging gently at her hands—a future that never came, a life that never bloomed.

Chapter Six
The Last Supper

They called it mercy weather—that strange warm wind that comes just before something terrible.

That Sunday, the house smelled of chicken broth, yeast, and apple peels. Outside, the first leaves had begun to fall. A celebration was coming—not a holiday, but something close enough. Roza was almost four months old, and Ana had finally agreed to let the two families gather in one place.

It was Vasyl's idea.

"They want to see her," he had said gently, standing behind Ana as she nursed the baby. "Your parents, mine. Just one afternoon. No arguing. No prayers."

Ana didn't answer right away. She looked down at Roza, her small mouth fluttering like a bird's against her skin. A fragile thing, this baby—but already stronger than anyone guessed.

"I won't hide her," she said finally. "But I won't pretend we're the same."

"They'll love her anyway."

"We'll see."

As the sun bent low against the sky, the table was neatly set with white cloth, linen napkins, and dishes passed down from Ana's mother. There were challah rolls, sprinkled with sesame seeds, still warm from the oven. Pickled beets. Cabbage with caraway. Roasted potatoes. And, on Halyna's insistence, a honey cake, shaped like a little Orthodox cross—just subtle enough to pass.

In the cradle beside the hearth, Roza cooed softly, wide awake and blinking at the light. She had begun to smile in the last few weeks—genuine smiles, not just sleepy twitching. When Vasyl leaned over her now, she reached out with a tiny hand and curled her fingers around his thumb.

"Look at that," he whispered. "She's learning to hold on."

Ana stood in the doorway, drying her hands on her apron and watching them.

She wanted to stop time. Just one hour. One evening, when they could eat, sing a little, pass Roza from lap to lap, and pretend that all the rumours—the soldiers, the borders, the fear stitched into every neighbour's eyes—were still a little farther away.

Her father arrived first, his coat too big on his thin shoulders, carrying a jar of stewed plums. He hugged Ana hesitantly, making her heart ache—like he was unsure whether he was still allowed to.

"Baruch Hashem," he said, bending over the cradle. "She's got your mouth. And your stubborn eyes."

Then came Halyna and Vasyl's two sisters—in—law, dressed in dark skirts and wool shawls, carrying a roast chicken and a jar of honey. They crossed themselves quickly before stepping over the threshold. Ana saw it, said nothing. She handed them tea, and when they didn't look her in the eye, she didn't force it.

By dusk, the house was full.

Someone started singing an old folk song. Someone else tapped out a rhythm on the table. Roza was passed around like a treasure. Even Ana's father and Halyna sat side by side for a moment, their hands both resting near the same teacup.

"You know," Vasyl said softly, as he came up behind Ana, "this could be something."

"This could be gone tomorrow," she answered.

He didn't argue.

Outside, the light was fading fast. Beyond the fields, no one could see the war yet—but they could feel it, like thunder far off. The radio whispered it. The news from Moscow was clipped and nervous, filled with Soviet propaganda and a fear of an upcoming war. Men spoke in half—sentences. Women kept their necessities packed.

Still, for this one night, Ana let herself believe in the table. In the baby's soft breath. In Vasyl's hand on her waist. In the way, two families who should never have fit together sat elbow to elbow, bound by bread and music and a little girl who didn't yet know the difference between them.

Roza let out a cry, not frightened—just loud, as if to say, I'm here.

Ana picked her up and cradled her close.

Her father turned to Halyna. "We don't yet know what kind of girl she'll grow into."

"She'll be good," Halyna replied. "She has strong hands."

"She has many names already," Ana added. "One in Yiddish, one in Ukrainian, and one that only I know."

Everyone looked at her then. But she didn't explain.

The laughter faded as the night deepened. Candles were lit. The older ones grew quiet, while the younger ones stayed up to play cards. No one mentioned politics or God. For once, they shared the same silence.

Later, when the guests had gone and the dishes were piled high, Ana stood at the window and looked across the fields. Roza slept in her arms, breath warm against her collarbone.

"She brought them together," she whispered.

And for a moment—just a moment-Ana imagined that love alone might be enough.

Beneath it all, she felt the thin and nearly invisible strong thread connecting past and present, binding them to an uncertain future. A fragile line holding tight, even as the world trembled just beyond the window.

Chapter Seven
Smoke on the Horizon
(Morning of June 22, 1941)

The night was thick with silence until a distant rumble stirred Ana awake. At first, she thought it was thunder—nature's low grumble rolling softly through the trees. But the sound deepened, spreading like a bruise across the sky. Heavier. Closer. Not thunder at all.

She sat up slowly, heart tightening. The room felt wrong—charged, as if the very walls were holding their breath.

Then Vasyl appeared in the doorway, his face pale, drawn, but calm.

"It's not thunder," he said quietly. "Cannons. They've begun."

Ana reached for the radio. A moment of static, and then a clipped voice cracked through:

"Attention. The state of war has been declared. The enemy has launched an attack."

The words hung in the air—heavy, raw, unreal.

Vasyl crossed the room and sat beside her, taking her hand. He didn't squeeze it. Just held it steady.

"We are from different worlds," he said softly. "Different faiths. Different names. But in the eyes of this storm… none of it matters. They see us both the same—others. Less than."

Ana's eyes searched his face. That truth—the one her parents had warned her about, the one they'd both tried to ignore—had finally stepped through the door.

"We carry different names," she whispered, "but the fear is one. Hope, too."

Outside, the cannons rolled again. No longer distant—closer than comfort could reach.

Vasyl stood. "We have to be ready. I'll go. To stand for us—for whatever's coming."

Ana's grip tightened. Her voice trembled, but didn't break.

"And Roza and I—where do we go?"

He looked at her. Then, at the cradle in the corner, where their daughter slept, her breath was soft and unaware.

"To my parents," Ana said. "For now."

Vasyl hesitated, then nodded.

She stepped closer and placed a hand on his cheek—still raw from the last shave.

"Promise you'll come back to her."

He looked down at Roza. Then at Ana.

"I'll come back to both of you," he said. Then, quieter—almost to himself: "I will come back."

Ana believed him. Not because it was true, but because she had to.

And beneath the roar of distant guns, she still felt it—barely, faintly—his heartbeat in her hand. A rhythm she knew like her own. As long as it beat, the world hadn't yet ended.

The train station smelled of wet earth and boiled potatoes. It was morning, but the heat already clung to the skin.

No one cried.

Women kissed their husbands with pressed lips. Boys puffed out their chests, pretending to be men. Older men shook hands harder than needed, as if pressure alone could hold something together.

Ana stood among them, Roza wrapped tightly against her breast, her tiny fist curled near Ana's collarbone.

Vasyl looked older—his shirt tucked too neatly, his eyes already far away. He held Roza once more, kissed her forehead, then looked at Ana.

"You'll write," she said.

"I'll try."

"I'll be safe. With your family."

He nodded.

The whistle shrieked. The crowd surged forward, a blur of movement and shouted names. Ana wanted to kiss Vasyl again—one more time. But he was already being pulled away. And just like that, he was gone. The train disappeared down the tracks, a black heartbeat swallowed by smoke.

Ana stood still, Roza warm against her chest, their two heartbeats now the only rhythm she could trust. One has barely begun—one breaking. The world was on fire. But for this moment, they still had each other.

Chapter Eight
The Last Snow

The first snow came before dawn, falling like ash over the fields and the crooked rooftops of the village. It brought a freezing silence that didn't comfort—only muffled—a stillness before something worse.

Ana stood in the doorway of her childhood home, a shawl pulled tightly around her shoulders, watching the pale flakes disappear into the ground. In her arms, Roza slept—just four months old—her breath warm against Ana's collarbone.

Since Vasyl left in June, nothing had been the same. The village had grown smaller, quieter. Then darker. Letters stopped coming. News arrived in whispers—about trains, roundups, camps. Entire families gone overnight.

The word Jew no longer meant neighbour or friend. It was something else now. Something hunted.

Inside the house, her parents moved in tense silence. Her mother stirred barley in a pot, and her father wiped down his tools without purpose. They were waiting, like everyone else. Waiting for the knock that hadn't yet come.

But something did come—not a knock at the door, but a soft tapping on the shutter. Ana moved quickly, cradling Roza against her chest as she glanced in the window and then pulled the door open. Halyna stood in the snow, her face red from the cold, her hands trembling.

She didn't ask to come in. She pushed past Ana into the room and unwrapped her coat, revealing a folded paper damp from her grip. Ana knew what it was before the older woman even spoke: a pohoronka, a Soviet soldier's death notice.

She handed it to Ana without a word. The seal was smudged, but the name was clear: "Vasyl Mykolayovych Holub. Killed in action. November 30, 1941".

Ana stared at it like it wasn't real. Her fingers traced the typewritten letters. Her lips slightly moved, trying to read the name of the place where he died-Pokrovka.

Roza stirred and giggled. Halyna looked at the baby—wide—eyed now, chewing on her fingers.

"She's the only part of him left," she said hoarsely. "And she's the only one we can save."

Ana looked up sharply.

"I have cousins in the next valley," the old woman went on. "One of their girls died last week. Typhus. No one outside the family knows. I'll say Roza is mine. No one will question. She's small. Pale. Her eyes… they could pass."

Ana clutched Roza tighter. "You want me to give her away?"

"I want her to live."

Ana turned to her parents. Her mother was crying silently, and her father sat in the corner, staring at the floor. No one said anything.

Outside, the snow was still falling—heavier now. A soft, relentless curtain between what was and what could no longer be. Inside her, something collapsed. She pressed her lips to Roza's forehead. The baby smelled of milk and soap. Of life. Of hope. Of Vasyl.

"You'll take care of her?" Ana whispered.

"As if she were mine," came the answer.

She didn't remember letting go. She just knew that suddenly her arms were empty. Halyna wrapped Roza in a thick woollen blanket and held her close.

"They won't look for a Ukrainian baby," she said quietly. "She has a chance."

She turned, opened the door, and stepped into the snow. Roza tucked in her coat. Ana stood at the window, watching until the figure disappeared into the white.

That night, her father carved a small wooden cross and pressed it into the frozen ground beneath the birch tree behind the house. Ana watched in silence, confused at first. Her father, a quiet man who still whispered the Shema before bed, held the cross in his calloused hands like something foreign.

"But we're not…" she began.

He looked at her with eyes aged far beyond their years.

"If someone comes," he said quietly, "they won't dig where there's a Christian cross."

A pause.

"And if she is already in God's arms," he added more softly, "then He will know who she is. Cross or no cross."

On the cross, he wrote: "Roza Vasylivna Holub. Born: March 24, 1941 Died: December 18, 1941."

The air was sharp and dry, the snow crunching like bone beneath their feet. A dog barked in the distance. Somewhere, a rooster called out, as if morning still meant something.

But inside Ana, something had been buried too—something more than a daughter, more than a future. The thread of hope, a tight string, snapped inside her. She wailed like a wounded animal, then sank to the floor by the door—motionless, silent. Her happy moments were in the past. Roza was gone. Vasyl was gone. Only silence remained and the snow.

Chapter Nine
The Roundup

The snow was bitterly—wind—blown and thin, as if even winter didn't want to stay. The air was filled with smoke, fear, and the faint, metallic smell of spilled blood.

The red Soviet banner had long since vanished from the town hall. In its place, silence. No speeches, no anthems, just the rustle of boots, foreign tongues, and fear. Every day brought rumours: entire Jewish neighbourhoods emptied. People were loaded into wagons and never seen again. Gunfire in the forests. Whole families swallowed whole.

Ana moved through it like someone already buried. One foot in front of the other. One breath at a time. One thought kept her alive: Roza is safe.

Tucked away in another village, under another name. Hidden in Vasyl's mother, Halyna's shawl. Smuggled across fields and through prayers, carried like a secret—the only thing Ana had left that was hers.

To the world, Roza was gone.

In December 1941, a grave was dug and filled. A wooden cross, carved by Nityaks for Holub, was hammered into frozen earth. Roza's name was etched by shaking hands. It was planted in sacred ground.

And then—quiet.

Until the knock.

It wasn't polite. It wasn't hesitant. It came like a hammer splitting wood, echoing inside Ana's parents' house with finality. Ana flinched. Her mother said nothing. Her father stared out the window, already somewhere else.

Ana stood. Miriam stood. Yitzhak stood.

Outside were three men. One German—tall, his face unreadable, the kind of calm that hides cruelty. Two Ukrainians stood behind him, local boys in patched coats. One wore the red—and—black trident of Bandera's army—the feared insignia of a ruthless militia. He couldn't have been older than eighteen.

The German spoke:

"Juden. Raus. Five minutes."

Jews. Out.

They had waited. Now they were collecting.

Ana didn't argue. She wrapped a scarf tightly around her hair, picked up her father's prayer book, and slipped her sewing thimble into her coat pocket. It was all she would take. Everything else was already lost.

Outside, the village had gathered. Hunched and hollow—eyed families shuffled toward the square like shadows: old men, young mothers, and children clutching dolls. The wind cut sharply between them.

Her neighbour whispered, "They shot the tailor in Lutsk. His wife, too."

Another added, "They say the trains go east. Or west. No one knows."

Rumors. Always rumours. But the gunshots were real.

Ana was pushed into a line. Her mother couldn't walk. She tried to carry her, but the soldiers pulled Miriam back. The Bandera boy laughed, the sound cruel and youthful. He pushed Miriam to the ground with the rest of the weak.

Ana tried to find her father, and this is when she saw the German officer watching her from the corner of her eye. He had pale, elegant hands—like a pianist's—and a coat stitched with eerie perfection. His calm was a mask, chilling in its quiet. She imagined him quoting Goethe while signing death orders.

He approached.

"You," he said in broken Russian. "You sew?" He mimed a small motion with his fingers—like drawing a threaded needle through a cloth, and pointed to the yellow star on her coat and laughed.

Ana quietly nodded, feeling the weight of his gaze on her hands and then her face. Something unreadable flickered in his eyes.

"So young," he murmured. "Too young to lose everything."

He turned away.

Ana was herded into a truck with two dozen others. This was the last time she saw her parents. Wooden slats pressed into her back. The air stank of fear and bodies. No one spoke. A baby whimpered once, then fell silent.

As the truck pulled away, she looked back. The house was shrinking, distant now—a place where she once sang lullabies. But Roza wasn't there. Roza was safe. The world would mourn her death. The grave would lie for her. The cross would hide her mother's truth. Ana-Ana would carry the weight of that lie wherever the truck was taking her. Because even in the face of annihilation, a mother doesn't give up. She gives everything else.

Chapter Ten
A Second Burial

She was barely twelve pounds when she left Ana's arms. Vasyl's mother, Halyna, carried her like contraband—not wrapped in blankets but in silence and dread. The winter of 1941 had turned the roads brittle, the trees hollow. Each time a patrol passed, she pressed the baby close enough to stop her breath. There was no room for sound, no room for mistakes.

The journey to her sister's farm near Horodok was long and unforgiving. But Halyna made it. She had already buried one child. She would not bury another.

They called Roza Larysa now. Just for a while. Just until it was safe.

Halyna fed her warm goat's milk by candlelight, held her through coughing fits, and whispered prayers through tears.

"This child is no less sacred," she told herself. "Even if we changed her name. God will not object."

But it wasn't heaven that frightened her. It was the farmer's wife who stared too long.

The neighbour who asked too casually, "How old is she now?"

The grocer, who tilted his head when Larysa wouldn't meet his eyes. The boys in armbands who passed through town, boots bright with polish and slogans about blood and soil spilling from their mouths like hymns.

By the spring of 1942, Halyna began to understand what she had been refusing to believe. Some secrets did not survive by hiding. They survived by ending. So she told the story no mother ever should. She said the baby, Larysa, had died. She said it was fever—quick, merciless, and silent.

She brought her back to her town to a priest who asked no questions. Nobody gathered. Halyna dug the grave. The cross was simple: "Roza Holub 1941–1942." There was no star—just her name, a rose above it, and the earth pressed flat above it.

The priest placed a hand on Halyna's shoulder, "God saved her, now my family will take care of her," he said softly and carried Roza away.

Halyna nodded, though she wasn't sure of it. The days after were blurred. She stayed with her sister, then moved back to her empty house. The war was eating through everything—homes, names, language. There was no room left for memory.

That night, Halyna sat at a kitchen table and cried, tears streaming down her cheeks. She packed all her belongings and put them in storage as if she never existed. She never spoke the names Roza or Larysa again.

"When it is all over, I will find Roza, and maybe Ana will be back,"-she sighed but did not cry, "When they are back home…"

And though spring came that year—tentative, stunted—it bloomed without Roza and Ana.

Chapter Eleven
Farewell

The cattle car reeked of sweat and fear, packed so tightly that Ana couldn't sit. Darkness pressed in from all sides, broken only by muffled sobs and the relentless clatter of iron wheels. The air was foul—thick with dust and dread, choking the spirit. Every breath was a battle. Outside, the world had vanished into the rattling echo of the train—a steel beast dragging them into the unknown.

Still, somewhere deep inside, she held a thread. Thin. Fraying. But still remembered her daughter's scar, the faint line on the soft, warm forehead. Ana had kissed it a hundred times. It had become a prayer. She saw Roza learning to walk through muddy fields, dipping Easter eggs in dye, and crossing herself clumsily the way Halyna might have taught her. She imagined her hair curling in the spring sun, her giggle wafting through the grass. These visions, tender and vivid, were a promise of undying Jewish and Ukrainian love, rooted in resilience.

Halyna, steadfast, was the symbol of the life Ana longed for, a tether to something pure and unbroken amid the hell she was forced into. She clung to this: that Roza was safe and that Halyna kept her safe. That somewhere, her daughter still existed—under another faith, with another life, but alive.

Even in the stink and crush of that train, Ana refused to forget who she was. She had nothing—no husband, no parents, no voice. But she still had Roza, if only in memory. If only in hope. She was still a mother.

Ana did not yet know what the next year would bring. Even in the suffocating darkness of the cattle car, surrounded by strangers and the unbearable stench of fear and death, she refused to lose herself. She remained human. She refused to let go of the hope that they would meet again.

That hope was her lifeline, a fragile thread keeping her soul intact amid the horrors of the journey. The relentless click—clack of the train wheels beneath her felt like a heavy heartbeat—steady, unforgiving—a cruel reminder of the journey she was trapped in.

She thought of Roza's scar again—a tiny mark on her forehead, a permanent reminder of life's wounds and its stubborn will to survive. That scar was a secret sign, a quiet defiance in a world determined to erase them.

The train's wheels thundered beneath her, steady and unyielding—a drumbeat of dread pounding through the wooden walls, a countdown to the unknown. Ana closed her eyes, letting the rhythm carry her through the darkness, clinging to the futures of Roza blooming in her mind—a silent promise that life would somehow find a way.

Were these memories real, or had her mind woven them from desperate hope? Did they exist beyond the darkness of the train and the cruelty ahead? Ana did not know. But holding onto these visions—whether truth or illusion—was the fragile thread that carried her through each unbearable day for the next three years.

Ana could not yet know what the future would bring, but she held onto the flickering hope that Roza was alive, somewhere beyond. That hope—fragile, uncertain, perhaps born from survival—gave her the strength to endure the horrors to come.

Only time would reveal the truth: upon her return in 1945, the village would greet her with silence beneath a heavy, gray sky. At the edge of the cemetery, a burnt church and two simple crosses stood side by side—weathered and cold—marking what everyone believed were the graves of Halyna and little Roza.

The wheels pounded like a heartbeat, steady and relentless—a rhythm that carried her away from everything she knew. Then, it stopped. The train shuddered to a halt. The heavy doors creaked open, and cold air rushed inside, stealing the warmth and humanity with it. The outside world was no longer the same; it was harsher, colder, and merciless.

Ana paused, the fear of the unknown pressing down on her shoulders. She did not yet know Roza's true fate; she only knew she must survive. She stepped forward into a world that no longer remembered her name—but still, she walked with her blue eyes fixed on the indifferent, cold white clouds above.

Chapter Twelve
The Camp

The train's iron doors slammed open, like a gunshot that shattered the fragile silence. The cold air hit Ana's face like a slap—biting, raw, filled with a metallic tang that clawed at her throat. Around her, a sea of bodies pressed tightly together, a living wall of trembling flesh and whispered prayers. The acrid smell of smoke curled upward from a lone, blackened chimney, a thin wisp twisting into the gray sky like the last breath of hope.

There was no chaos—only a dreadful, suffocating stillness, broken by the faintest murmurs of Yiddish prayers and the quick, uneven breaths of mothers holding children too close.

Ana caught fragments of their whispered pleas: "Sh'ma Yisroel, Adonoi Eloheinu, Adonoi Echad…"

A mother clutched her baby tightly against her chest, the child's weak whimper swallowed by the cold. The woman limped, pain etched deep in every step, her face pale but proud. She moved slowly, resigned, as if each movement was an act of defiance against the darkness creeping closer.

The sudden bark of orders shattered the fragile quiet. "Workers here! Others over there!"

The crowd jolted, the line dividing salvation from death. Ana's chest tightened, her breath hitched. Everyone's fate was balanced on the edge of those cold commands.

At the top of the clearing, between two guarded columns—one leading deeper into the camp, one toward the unknown—stepped a man: tall, gaunt, and terrifyingly calm. His uniform was pitch black, spotless, with cruel insignias that gleamed under the morning light. His pale face was almost skeletal, his lips were thin and tight, and his eyes looked like cold steel—merciless and calculating. He carried the scent of leather and stale tobacco, but beneath it lay something darker, a sickly sweetness that made Ana's stomach churn. His eyes scanned the crowd with clinical precision until they landed on Ana.

"Papers," he commanded, voice low but sharp enough to cut.

Hands shaking, Ana produced the tattered document. The officer looked at her and then examined the paper slowly, as if savouring the power he held.

Then, with a slight nod, he pointed: "Worker. You."

Her legs obeyed before her mind caught up. Behind her, the mother with the baby was singled out by the officer's cold gaze. A cruel gesture sent the woman toward the waiting column.

Ana saw the horror in her eyes—silent, raw, desperate. The woman limped forward, clutching her child, each step a whispered farewell.

A soft sound came from the crowd—a word, a death sentence disguised in silence: "Showers."

But there were no showers. They were the gates of oblivion.

The smoke from the chimney thickened, blotting out the sky and creeping down like a suffocating fog. The air grew heavier and harder to breathe. Ana's nostrils flared, the bitter stench of burning flesh stabbing at her senses.

She forced her eyes closed, clutching the tiny ember of hope inside her. The undying hope that Roza was alive, somewhere beyond this deadly life. Around her, the world was crumbling into ash. But Ana refused to let her flicker of hope die—not while Roza might still breathe, somewhere beyond the smoke.

Chapter Thirteen
The Selection

The line shuffled forward beneath the watchful eyes of the guards. Ana's body ached from exhaustion and cold, the rough wooden boards of the barracks a faint memory against her skin. At night, she had curled with others in the cramped quarters, the air thick with the smell of sweat, fear, and damp wood. The thin straw beneath her offered little comfort.

When the order came, she rose with the others, her legs stiff and trembling. Outside, the sky was a dull gray, the fences looming like silent sentinels topped with barbed wire that seemed to cut the pale light itself. Crossing that fence meant crossing into another world—one ruled by whispered commands and unspeakable cruelty.

Her heart pounded as the officer's gaze landed on her. Without a word, his hand snapped, and she was pulled from the crowd.

"You," he said sharply in German. "Here."

No kindness. No mercy. No hope.

Ana swallowed the lump in her throat and followed, passing under the barbed wire to the other side, where she would serve in the shadows, invisible and expendable. She was nobody—just another worker, another pair of hands to clean, to carry, to obey.

Inside the heavy, gray stone house just beyond the camp's perimeter, the air was colder in a different way—sterile, faintly perfumed with pipe tobacco and polish, mingled with the trace of leather and dust. The windows were curtained in heavy damask, the thick carpets muted the steps, and the walls were lined with faded oil portraits of sombre men in military uniforms.

Near the window sat the officer's wife, her fingers deftly working the delicate threads of a needlepoint. The canvas was alive with colour—a single rose, full bloom, unfolding its petals with painstaking precision. The soft pinks and deep reds seemed almost to glow against the dull gray of the room.

Her posture was relaxed, but her eyes held a distant sadness, as if the flower she stitched was a fragile hope she was trying to hold onto in a world unravelling around her. When her gaze briefly met Ana's, there was a flicker of something unreadable—curiosity? Compassion? Guilt?

"Du wirst hier bleiben," the officer said, nodding toward Ana.

The wife's delicate hands never stopped moving, but her eyes watched Ana with a quiet intensity, as if silently measuring the girl who had been brought to this place and her home.

A boy, perhaps twelve or thirteen, sat nearby at a small table, nervously twisting a chess piece between pale fingers. His face was too still, his eyes too cautious—eyes already knowing too much for one so young.

The officer himself remained in the doorway, tall and severe, his uniform immaculate. His dark eyes met Ana's with a hardness that chilled her, but beneath it flickered something dangerous, something curious and calculating. Educated and refined, yes, but here, refinement was a weapon, cold and merciless.

The distant smell of smoke drifted in, the faint plume rising from the camp's single chimney like a shadow behind the polished silence of this house.

As Ana crossed the threshold, the clang of the barbed wire fence echoed in her ears. She was nobody here. But the rose lingered in her mind—stubborn, delicate, alive.-a flicker of hope in the darkness.

Chapter Fourteen
Hollowed

Every morning, Ana slipped through the side entrance from the camp, shoulders hunched against the cold, the mud clinging to her thin shoes. She scrubbed floors, folded laundry, fetched coal, and dusted the portraits of stern ancestors. Her hands—raw and cracked—moved like they had forgotten they once created beauty. Once, they threaded flowers on dresses. Once, they stitched dreams into thread.

The officer rarely spoke to her. At least, not at first.

She became accustomed to the silence of the house—the muffled voices, the clink of silverware, the rhythmic click of the wife's needlepoint frame. The rose was nearly complete now, its petals almost fully unfurled. Ana watched it grow day by day, a strange witness to the slow bloom of something fragile amid so much stillness. It became, absurdly, a measure of time.

The wife looked through her as she no longer existed. The boy stopped twisting his chess piece.

One evening, Ana was sent to clean the study. The door closed behind her. She didn't hear the key turn, but she felt it—like a shift in the air.

He was already inside. Sitting by the fire.

"Mädel, girl," he said—not unkindly. The way someone might call a dog. "Come here."

Her feet stayed rooted, but her body moved. She knew better than to disobey. The warmth of the room prickled against her skin, too sharp after the icy air outside.

He offered her a glass of schnapps. She did not drink. He laughed—softly, bitterly. A cultured man: music, art, languages. But his power wasn't in what he knew. It was in what he owned.

And here, he owned everything—even her silence.

She remembered the first time his hand touched her wrist. Not roughly. Not violently. Just deliberately.

She thought of Roza in that moment. Of her soft hand curled around Halyna's. Of the little wooden cross she'd worn at her christening. Of the imagined sound of her footsteps in a schoolyard—running toward a life Ana could never see. It kept her breathing. It kept her body separate from her self.

What happened next was not spoken of. Not screamed. Not resisted. Resistance was futile—and for whom? For what? Another night. Another body. Hers.

She left the study numb. Not broken. Detached.

The wife never asked why her eyes were red, her hands wrapped her body tighter, and her shoulders slouched as if to cover shame. The rose, now complete, hung in a simple gold frame above the piano. Its bloom stared down like an accusation. Or a witness.

The boy wouldn't meet her gaze anymore.

Later, in the barracks, Ana lay on the hard planks, shoulder to shoulder with the others. She did not cry. She did not sleep. She listened to the breath of the women beside her, the soft moans in dreams, the murmurs in Yiddish of mothers and children long gonc.

She whispered nothing into the dark, not even Roza's name. But in her heart, she held the image of a little girl playing in the snow, the pale winter sun catching the pink tip of her nose. She remembered the colour of her coat. She remembered her laugh.

The officer could take her body, her silence, her wilted skin. But not that. Not her memory. Not her love that she gave to Vasyl, Roza, and others.

Chapter Fifteen
Swallowed

There was no time in the camp—only the rhythm of orders, the shuffle of feet, the hiss of the wind through barbed wire. Ana moved like a thread pulled through cloth—tight, linear, invisible.

Each day, she crossed through the gate to the house and returned before nightfall to the barracks, where bodies were stacked on planks like fabric bolts in her father's old tailor shop. The smell was sour—sweat, decay, smoke, fear. But there were human things, too: a whisper of Yiddish lullabies, a shared bread crust, a needle tucked into a hem, passed hand to hand like contraband.

The women had stopped counting the days. They marked time by who was gone.

Ana did not tell anyone when her body began to betray her.

At first, it was just a weight in her lower belly. A shift. A soreness. Then came the bleeding. Silent, discreet. In the dark, she curled into herself, teeth clenched against the pain. She bit down on her sleeve so that no sound would escape. The night pressed in. She didn't cry. She didn't beg. She just… endured.

An older woman named Malka—bones sharp under papery skin, eyes still alive—noticed. Malka said nothing. She simply pressed a cloth into Ana's hand one morning, coarse but clean, and sat beside her that night, her back against the cold wall of the barracks. They didn't speak. They didn't need to.

When the pain came again, sharper, final, Malka held her hand. She didn't ask questions. She didn't offer comfort. Just presence. That was enough.

Ana lost the child between breaths, between roll calls, between one day and the next.

It was not her first loss. But this time, she felt betrayed by her own weakened and battered body for getting her into this mess and then trying to clean it by sucking the last drop of life still left in her veins.

She never said the word—pregnant. Never dared think of a future with a child in it. She hadn't given it a name, hadn't imagined its face. It wasn't a baby, not in this place, not in this life. It was something taken from her before she could choose to hold it.

In the days after, she moved slower. Bent deeper. The officer's wife didn't notice—she was working on a new rose now, this one with thorns.

Ana watched the red petals form with a kind of numb awe. Even pain could be stitched into beauty. Or was it because of it?

Back in the barracks, Malka combed Ana's hair with her fingers and told her about her own daughters. Then one night, with the wind rattling through the slats, she leaned in closer.

"I had three," she said in Yiddish, voice low. "Rivka. Toba. Miriam."

Ana blinked.-Miriam, her mother's name. The coincidence stirred something profound but unspeakable.

Malka shifted and reached beneath the straw—stuffed mattress. She pulled out a small, cloth bundle, no larger than a folded handkerchief. Her fingers worked the knot slowly, reverently.

Inside, carefully folded, was a single photograph—faded, worn, its edges curled from time and damp. Three girls stood proudly in front of a tidy shop with a striped awning, neatly dressed in their best clothes, frozen in time. The corner of the image was torn, and the name of the shop behind them had vanished into the past.

"My husband left first," Malka said. "To New York. We too had everything—tickets to Italy and then to New York, affidavits, even a cousin waiting there. But my widowed father..." She shook her head. "He became gravely ill. So we stayed. I thought there would be time..."

She touched the photograph gently, her finger hovering over the smudged space where the shop name had been.

"I've kept this hidden since the ghetto. They were gone, one by one, and I couldn't save them. None of them. This is the only thing that is left. If I lose this-" she trailed off, voice suddenly thin, silent tears streaming down the sunken cheeks.

Ana didn't respond. There was nothing to say. But she reached out and closed Malka's hand gently over the photo, pressing it to her chest.

They sat side by side like that for a long time, with the sound of distant boots outside and the low murmur of breath all around them.

The stars outside the barrack window—what little they could see—remained indifferent. But Ana felt something small and vital passed between them, like a thread from one hand to another.

She thought of Roza. Her sacrifice had not been in vain. That hope—that imagined life—was still inside her, like an ember. It hadn't gone out.

In the camp, everything was taken: names, bodies, time. But not memory, not belief, not sacrifice. She would carry them, like her defiance. Quiet, invisible, permanent.

Chapter Sixteen
Empty Space

It happened between night and dawn, in the sliver of silence just before the guards shouted roll call. Malka was gone.

There were no cries, no drama, just a stillness that hadn't been there the day before. Her body curled like a question mark, hands folded across her belly as if she had simply gone to sleep and decided not to wake.

Ana had seen too much to be shocked. But something inside her—small, deeply human—shivered.

The barracks were already stirring. Wood creaked. Women rose, half—asleep, tugging on rags and boots. No one said much. They never did. Words had become rationed things, spent only when necessary. Grief was quieter than hunger here.

Ana sat beside Malka's body and looked at her face. The tension was gone. Her jaw was soft. The lines around her mouth had eased. In death, she looked younger. Less guarded. Ana reached out and smoothed a wisp of Malka's gray hair behind her ear. It was the smallest gesture, but it felt immense. Ana did not cry. She had no tears left.

They came for the body mid—morning while Ana was at the house—two men in striped uniforms who looked past everything. She wasn't the first, and she wouldn't be the last. They did not say her name. They lifted her gently, efficiently.

Later, in the line outside, she touched the cloth pouch Malka had shown her—the photograph folded inside. She had stitched it carefully into the waistband of her striped trousers and carried it close—a hidden memory, a talisman.

She pressed her fingers against it and whispered, "Zay gezunt." Be well.

Even now, it mattered. Malka was gone, and the space she had taken up was so small, yet Ana felt it like a cold wind in her ribs. There were no graves, no names carved in stone, just the living, carrying the dead inside them.

But memory lingered. That night, Ana dreamt of a hand brushing hers, of voices humming in a language the camp had not yet extinguished—a lullaby, a prayer. In the dream, Malka did not look old. She sat on a chair near a window overlooking an endless blue sea, hands full of thread, pulling life back together stitch by stitch. Her daughters, laughing, smiling, and eating cannolis, were sitting beside her—together at last.

Ana woke up with the taste of salt on her lips. She looked out at the fence and the sky beyond it. There was no moon.-only stars, half—visible through smoke. Malka was gone. But something of her remained, folded inside Ana—not just memory, but something warm against her skin.

It was the little cloth pouch, stitched tight and hidden in the slit in the waistband of her striped trousers, worn smooth from touch. Inside the photograph. Three girls, three daughters. They were hers now. A secret. A promise. Each time her fingers brushed the fabric of the pouch, something flickered through the numbness. Not hope, exactly. Something quieter. Fiercer. A vow stitched into her. The will to remember. To live.

There were no funerals. Only footsteps. Only breath. Only empty spaces. And Ana would carry Malka. In silence. In the photograph. In the hush between waking and sleeping.

Malka had lost her daughters. But now, Ana thought, she would carry them, too. Roza was not alone anymore. Ana had more daughters now—three she had never known, and one she had given away.

The pouch pressed gently at her side, and the picture warmed against her body. It was enough—not a grave, but something close—a shrine made of loss, memory, and survival.

Chapter Seventeen
Stopped

Time lost its name in the camp. There were no Mondays. No seasons. Only tasks. Hours. Footsteps. Only the rhythm of survival. Ana moved like film through a projector—one frame bleeding into the next. Scrub the stairs. Peel the potatoes. Mend the cuff. Polish the boots. Bleach the collars. The Herr in the study. Walk back through the gate. Get searched. Sleep on wood. Wake up. Begin again.

The house was warm. The barracks were not. In the house: white linen, ticking clocks, the scent of starch and lemon oil. The Frau with her long, nimble fingers, working roses into fabric—blossoms that would never wilt.

Once, she pricked her finger and bled. Ana caught her breath.

The Frau wiped the blood away and laughed. "Even roses bite."

The man was colder. Always watching. Never loud. Never messy. Even his violence was quiet—folded into corners, hidden behind closed doors. It always happened on time, on schedule. That almost made it worse. Each time, Ana returned to the barracks wordless.

Malka had once whispered, "This place unweaves the human out of you, thread by thread."

But Ana kept one thread tight inside her. A name. A rose. Roza. She imagined the sound of her laughter. A girl's breath fogging a window. A small hand grabbing bread with both fists. A cross on her chest. A scar on her forehead—tiny, like a secret. Ana imagined her alive.

Every day, more faces disappeared, and the barracks thinned. Some marched out and never returned, and others faded in their sleep like candle smoke.

Ana stitched shirts. Skirts. Winter coats with padded linings she would never wear. Sometimes, in the hem, she slipped a single stitch in the shape of a rose. The Frau never noticed.

And then… One morning, a rumble. Far off. Like distant thunder rolling over dry earth. It stopped the women mid—step. One turned her head toward the east. Another looked at the sky. A third whispered, "Cannons."

No one dared speak it aloud, but Ana felt it in her bones: the rhythm had changed. The reel was skipping. Something had torn in the sky. That night, she stepped outside to empty a bucket. The sky glowed red at the edges. The guard barked, but even his voice trembled. The smell of burning lingered, as always. But beneath it, something new: ash disturbed by wind.

Liberation hadn't come. Not yet. But the world was moving. And Ana—who had stopped counting time—suddenly counted one more day. Not survived.

Endured. The sound of cannons still echoed in her ribs when she laid her head down.

Chapter Eighteen
The Fallen Threat

It began with silence. Not peace—silence, brittle and sharp, like glass stretched too thin. No footsteps echoed through the tiled hallway. No shouting orders. No clatter of boots. Even Frau's voice, once sharp and exact as a sewing pin, had gone quiet.

Ana noticed first in the kitchen. The kettle remained cold. The cutlery drawer hung open, half—full. The linens hadn't been washed. The uniforms were sitting in the study. Alone. Ana was not called in there for some time.

And then, the roses. Frau's embroidery had once been her ritual. The hoop was always near, the colored threads like veins running from her fingers into the cloth—a garden blooming in thread. Now the hoop lay discarded on the table. The half—finished rose sagged in its outline, a single petal curled and incomplete. A needle, once so meticulously handled, stuck crooked into the cloth—forgotten. Ana touched the thread with her thumb. It snagged.

Upstairs, drawers opened and slammed shut. A suitcase groaned under the weight. Herr hadn't spoken in days. He paced from room to room, collecting documents, cufflinks, and the revolver. His uniform hung on the door, its silver buttons catching the last of the winter light.

Outside, the smoke still curled from the distant chimney, but it was thinner now, less consistent—as if even the furnaces were losing their purpose.

Inside the barracks, whispers passed from woman to woman: "They're leaving."

"Burning records."

"Some guards are already gone."

"Trucks rolled out last night."

And yet, the gate still stood. The wires still crackled. The German Shepherds still barked.

On her final day in the house, Ana was sent to dust the sitting room. It felt like entering a mausoleum. The velvet chairs sat untouched. The clock had stopped. The study was empty.

The rose embroidery on the Frau's frame had begun to unravel—a strand of crimson thread hanging like a torn vein. Ana touched it. The Frau appeared behind her, sudden and strange. Her face was bare. Paler than Ana had ever seen it. Her hair was undone. She looked… not younger, but less real. Like someone dreaming themselves into the world.

She said nothing. Then, with slow and trembling hands, she picked up the embroidery, stared at it, and tore it from the frame in a single, sharp motion. The unfinished rose dropped to the floor.

Ana bent to pick it up, but the Frau waved her away.

"There won't be time," she said, and her voice cracked on the word.

That evening, the gate was left ajar. Ana crossed it without being stopped. No one searched her. No dog barked. The silence was deafening.

And then the sound of another army came for the first time in years. Tires on gravel. Shouted voices she didn't understand. And then… Russian. Liberation arrived like thunder— Not in sound, but in pressure. Heavy in the chest. Like the air before a storm.

Ana stood at the edge of the camp, where the garden of roses bloomed in the gated house. The only thing left was a tangle of thread in her pocket—crimson and gold—the remnants of someone else's idea of beauty.

She turned her face to the smoke—the smell of burning wood, not flesh. And breathed it in. Again. And again.

Chapter Nineteen
Remains

The train moved slower this time. There were windows now—cracked, smeared, but real. Ana sat by one and kept her eyes on the gray blur of landscape sliding past. Her hands rested in her lap. Someone had given her clothes: a worn wool skirt, a man's shirt too large for her narrow frame, and boots that blistered her heels. Beneath it all, the striped fabric of the camp still touched her skin. She hadn't been able to remove it completely. Not yet.

She didn't speak. Neither did the other passengers. Each face had its own hollow geography—a landscape of hunger, of absence, of survival without celebration. They were all travelling back to places that had already buried them.

The countryside rolled out under a thin mist of early spring. Trees that had once marked paths now stood skeletal and unfamiliar. Chimneys stood like gravestones. Some villages had disappeared altogether—burned down, hollowed out, replaced by scorched fields or silence.

When the train stopped, Ana stepped out alone. No one was waiting.

The walk to the village was long. Mud sucked at her boots. Her legs ached. She passed people, but no one stopped. Her name had become irrelevant. She was a stranger now, even to herself.

The village still stood—what was left of it.

An older woman looked at her as she saw a ghost, shook her head in disbelief and mumbled under her breath, "They are all gone, Holubs, Nityaks…"

The wooden houses hunched together like old women in mourning. The well she remembered as a girl was still there, the rope frayed but intact. A rooster called out from somewhere, its voice sharp against the muffled stillness. Time had moved on here, but without healing.

She made her way to the cemetery first. Her feet knew the way. She found them side by side: two weathered and gray wooden crosses with simple names etched by a trembling hand: "Roza Holub, 1941–1942. Halyna Holub, 1882–1942."

Ana sank to her knees. She placed her hand on the frozen earth. It felt hard, final.

The sky above was low and metallic. Not a single bird sang. Silence pressed in around her, like the silence of the train, the silence of the chimneys, the silence of the house where roses were stitched.

There were no tears. Just breathe. In and out. A steady heartbeat of a broken heart. Hope held, hope lost.

She imagined Roza's hand in Halyna's—the little cross on her chest, the painted Easter eggs, the lullaby Ana hummed but never sang. She remembered the weight of that choice, the sound of thunder mistaken for a storm, the scream she never let out when she gave her daughter away to be saved.

And now—a grave. A name. And two dates. But Ana… Ana did not believe it. Not fully. Some part of her—the same part that carried her through the nights in the barrack, the part that bled and did not die—refused to believe that Roza's name etched in wood was the end.

Maybe it was a survival instinct. Maybe it was madness. Maybe it was love.

She stood. She would not stay here. There was nothing left to bury. The future did not grow from graves. She would go. Anywhere. Elsewhere. Italy, perhaps. Where no one knew her name or her silence or her sins.

But in her pocket, she would carry that last thread. Crimson. A rose, unfinished. In her other pocket—a pouch with the photograph of the three girls who would make it to Italy this time. And in her chest—the unbearable ache of what a mother never truly buries.

Chapter Twenty
Crimson

Ana did not scream. She doubled over in a stranger's barn, alone and shaking. The world outside slowly bloomed into postwar spring, while inside her, winter let go of one last remnant.

The blood came fast, hot and thin, staining the little nest she made in the hay. Her fingers gripped the straw beneath her, pressing through years of hunger and silence. Her teeth clenched, but no sound escaped. Pain, she knew. Pain had lived in her bones for so long that it no longer needed an invitation.

It ended in darkness. When Ana woke, she was in a hospital. Clean walls. Sharp light. The silence of cotton and alcohol. The first thing she saw was a flower—in a vase, next to her bed—a rose. It was in full bloom, almost artificial in its perfection.

A nurse came. Then a doctor. They spoke with the gentle efficiency of people who had seen too much.

"You lost a lot of blood," the doctor said as a matter of fact. "You were already very weak. It was lucky they found you when they did."

Ana turned her face away.

He hesitated. Then, more softly: "There won't be more children. I'm sorry."

No reply. Just a long, quiet exhale. She stared at the rose in the vase. She thought of blood—not just this blood, but the other, the older one. The bloodline. The tiny heartbeat once inside her. Lost.

"Twice," she thought. "Twice now."

Roza was dead. This child never lived. The war had taken everything. It carved her open, hollowed her out. Now, she was free—and it felt like death.

The next morning, she rose. Still weak. Still pale. But upright. She left the hospital with a thread of bandage still around her wrist. She took nothing but her name—what was left of it—and a promise stitched deep in her silence: She would never return here. Not to this land. Not to this war. Not to this grave of years.

Italy. The sea. A place where she was no one. She walked to the train station alone. She didn't cry. She hadn't in years. But as the wheels turned and the fields rolled past, she whispered something to herself—not a prayer, not quite. A song, almost. In broken Yiddish. A lullaby. For the children who had lived, and the ones who never did. And for herself, the woman who was told would no longer be able to give life, but still—somehow—alive.

Chapter Twenty-One
Ruins

The road out of the village curved through ruins and thawing mud. Spring crept up through the bones of the earth, but the towns still looked shelled, gray, shivering. War had moved on. Its shadow hadn't.

Ana walked alone. Her shawl was thin, and her boots were too large. In the distance, a train whistled low—a tired sound, like a breath let out too late. At the edge of a ruined town stood a makeshift transit station. The brick was crumbling, and the windows were gone. A sign still hung crooked above the doorway, the letters half—burned and unreadable.

She stepped into the crowd of displaced people—women with canvas bags, children clutching bread crusts, and men who no longer stood tall. Everyone was waiting to leave, to begin elsewhere, or just to keep moving.

A cordon of wire separated another group. Guarded. Silent. She glanced across without meaning to—and stopped. Wagner. He stood in a line of prisoners. Stripped of rank. Jacket unbuttoned. Beard coarse and uneven. His hands with nails broken, dirty. But his eyes—still sharp. They met hers. Recognition struck them both in an instant. His face twitched. Something passed through it: disbelief, then calculation, then the first faint breath of remorse.

Ana didn't blink. She stepped toward the cordon. A guard barked something in Russian, but didn't stop her. She stood across from Wagner, no more than two meters away. The wire between them sagged.

He opened his mouth—to speak, perhaps. Or lie. Ana spat. Deliberate. Wordless. The spit hit the dust near his boots, dark against the pale dirt. Wagner flinched—barely, but enough. He closed his mouth. Looked down.

Ana didn't move. A soft hand came to rest on hers. She turned. An older woman stood beside her. Thin face. Hollowed eyes. But her grip was warm, steady.

"That one?" the woman asked, voice quiet.

Ana nodded.

The woman's eyes didn't leave him. Her voice was calm, almost tender: "He will never hurt you or anyone else again. Never ever again."

The words hung in the air like a verdict. Ana let out a breath she hadn't known she was holding. Her chest ached, but it didn't collapse.

The train hissed. A soldier began shouting names in clipped syllables. A door creaked open. The crowd started to shift, gather, and move.

Ana stepped back from the wire. Wagner hadn't looked up again. She left him there—in his silence, in his threadbare coat, in the line of men waiting for their own uncertain judgment.

She did not look back.

The train rocked forward, slow and groaning, wheels catching rhythm. Ana sat by the window. The same older woman was beside her now, hands clasped in her lap, eyes closed but not asleep.

Outside, fields slid by, ruptured and grey—green, half—thawed. Smoke rose from chimneys again. Someone planted potatoes in a broken yard. Inside, the carriage smelled of damp wool, iron, and earth.

Ana closed her eyes. She remembered the other train—the one that had taken her to the camp— and how the wheels also sounded like a heartbeat. Not hers. The train's. Steady. Relentless. Unfeeling. This rhythm was different. Still heavy. Still uncertain. But not the same. Not death. Life unknown.

She didn't know where the tracks would take her. Not really. Italy, maybe. Or farther. To a city without memory, without smoke in the sky, without her daughter's name whispered like a wound.

She didn't know what she would do there, or who she would be. But she was moving. And the train—this one—beat with the rhythm of possibility. A slow, fractured hope. A pulse she could almost believe was her own.

Chapter Twenty-Two
Scarf of Roza

Italy was a place of muted colours and sudden bursts of light—laundry lines snapping in the wind, lemon trees blooming against peeling walls, voices rising like music then vanishing into silence. It smelled of roasted chestnuts, warm fabric, salt, and distant rain.

Ana worked in a tailor's shop tucked into a narrow alley just past a modest piazza. It belonged to a quiet man named Signor Battisti, who took in repairs and alterations and allowed Ana to use a table by the window for her own work. She never asked for big wages. He never asked for her story.

Her fingers had become strong again. They moved with care and precision, even when her heart felt slow. Some days she sewed in silence, others she hummed old Yiddish lullabies, the melodies soft and circular, looping back on themselves like threads refusing to break.

Customers came and went—mostly women. Stout mothers with grown daughters bickering over sleeve length, children twirling in half—hemmed skirts, and sharp—eyed matrons who wanted mourning dresses taken out now that the worst was behind them.

One girl—maybe seven—once spilled a bag of buttons across the floor. She squealed with delight, chasing them like fireflies. Her mother shouted after her in rapid Italian, waving a shoe and exclaiming that she would "drag her home by the ears." Ana watched with quiet wonder. The girl was unafraid. Even in her tears, she was loved, held, scolded—alive.

"She has a mother," Ana thought. "And she still has time."

That afternoon, Ana returned to her embroidery. She had been working on a scarf for weeks, a long and quiet labour. It began with a rose—delicate, layered, stitched in crimson thread. Around it, she wove four faces: a child with eyes wide as spring, a young woman with braids and wonder, a mother with grief pressed into the corners of her mouth, and an old woman with wise eyes and a mouth like a seam.

The scarf was not for sale yet. On one edge, she embroidered a small symbol—a hand cradling a broken heart, a single blue tear stitched beneath. It was something she had once seen in a Jewish cemetery. A mother's grief that was made permanent in stone now lived in thread.

And always, as she sewed, she remembered the German woman—the officer's wife—who had once sat in a warm parlour, stitching roses while smoke curled outside. Her embroidery had been neat, perfect, unaware. Ana hadn't understood, then, why that image remained. Now she did. It was the act—not the rose, but the making of it. Creating life when death cursed the living, and hope was lost, was an act of defiance, an act of remembering, and an act of asking for forgiveness.

One morning, the door chimed, and a tall man entered—elegant and reserved, his coat impeccable but his shoes dusty from travel. His hair had gone silver at the temples. He walked with the grace of someone used to being listened to, but his eyes were tired, as if they had stopped hoping to find what they'd once lost.

He wore a simple, almost invisible, gray kippah. Ana's fingers froze mid—stitch.

He was escorted by the American woman—the one who had come days earlier and admired the scarf, her eyes full of something she hadn't said aloud.

"This is the one I mentioned," the woman said, gesturing toward Ana's work.

The man approached. He examined the scarf without touching it. His gaze lingered on the rose, the faces, the small tear.

Then, very softly, he said: "Wunderschön." And then: "Danke."

The word struck her like a blow.

Ana's body tensed, her heart jerking sideways in her chest. Danke. That word, that sound—it had lived in the mouths of men who carried rifles, who shouted orders, who herded children into rooms that were filled with smoke.

Her hand faltered. Her eyes narrowed. He saw it—the change in her, the tightening in her posture. He lowered his gaze.

Softly, he said again: "Grazie."

It wasn't just a translation. It was a quiet apology.-a gesture of understanding. Ana gave a small nod, her jaw still set, but something inside her softened—slightly.

He folded the scarf with reverent hands, not as one who owned it, but as someone who recognized its weight while the American woman paid for it.

As he turned to go, he paused. His eyes met hers again. He didn't speak, but there was something unspoken between them—perhaps recognition of pain shaped by the same fire, though worn differently.

Later, the tailor chuckled when the door closed behind him: "A kind man," he said. "His wife, his daughters—gone. But he still sees people. Still listens. Not many like that."

Ana didn't answer. She picked up her needle again, but her hands didn't move right away.

She sat, staring at the scarf now gone, the table empty before her. Through the open window came the sound of bells ringing from a nearby church and the scent of baking bread. Two children ran past, chasing each other with laughter that filled the street.

And in the distance, a lullaby stirred in her memory—half in Yiddish, half in silence. And then—in Ukrainian.

She did not sing it aloud, only mouthed the words as her needle stilled, as if the thread itself could carry the tune, "Oyfn pripetshik brent a fayerl…"-a fire burns on the hearth… "Spi, moye dytya…"-sleep, my child…

The words wound through her chest like smoke through rafters—remembered not from the world, but from the bones. Not just for Roza. Not only for what was lost. But for herself—the girl who once listened, the mother who once sang, the woman now learning to breathe. The woman who was learning, slowly, to live again.

Later that evening, Ana stepped outside to catch the last of the golden light. The piazza rang with voices. A woman was arguing with a butcher. Two boys chased pigeons. A girl played clapping games with her sister, their laughter shrill and full of delight.

Somewhere, a bell rang for vespers.

Ana thought of the scarf, which was now finished and sold. Of Roza. Of the life that had ended and the one that might not have. Of the man's eyes. The dust on his shoes.

She went back inside and started the new scarf, new threads. Not just the rose. Not just the faces. Not just the flower. Not just the memory. The whole thing—thread, faces, sorrow, and song—a grieving mother who carried her sorrow through ash and silence.

She folded it carefully, once more, and placed it in the box. One day, someone will come for it. But tonight, it belonged only to her.

Chapter Twenty Three
Shared Ghosts

The late afternoon light filtered softly through the shop's dusty windows, casting warm, dappled patterns on the worn wooden floor. Ana sat at her small worktable, her fingers tracing the delicate embroidery of the rose blossoming in the scarf's center. Around it were four faces—a child, a youth, an adult, and an elder—a quiet homage to the circle of life.

David stood across from her, watching without speaking. He had been returning to the shop for over a week now—under the pretense of adjusting a collar, replacing a button, measuring a cuff. But they both understood it wasn't about the clothes.

It was the silence he came for. The stillness. Her presence.

He brought small things—never flowers, never anything too bright—but once, a worn poem tucked into his coat lining, and often, a paper bag with fresh cannoli from the bakery at the alley's end. Always dusted with powdered sugar.

"They remind me of something from childhood," he'd said once, without explaining further.

They rarely spoke of the past, but it lived between them like an open drawer—its contents quietly visible.

They drank tea in chipped porcelain cups—black, bitter, Russian. Ana brewed it strong, the way Vasyl had liked it. David never asked for a sweetener.

Some silences stretched long. Others were filled with quiet work—hemming, pinning, the soft thrum of fabric folding like pages between them.

One afternoon, as they shared tea and cannoli at the edge of twilight, David finally spoke, voice low, steady: "I escaped Germany on one of the last ships before everything collapsed. My wife and daughters… they were supposed to follow on another ship. But it never arrived."

Ana's breath caught. She set her cup down slowly. "I lost my Roza," she said. "And Vasyl. My husband was killed at the start of the war. And my little girl… No more. But I always carry her with me."

She looked down, then back at him. "I never imagined saying that out loud again."

David didn't offer comfort. He only reached forward and, with quiet care, touched her fingers—resting lightly, not holding, not urging. Just presence. Her hand stayed, quiet as breath.

The next day, he brought her a worn book of psalms, the leather soft with age. "It's my father's," he said. He used to keep it in his coat. He gave it to me before I left."

Ana opened it gently, her fingers lingering on the Hebrew letters as if touching something alive. She looked up and nodded.

Over the following days, their rhythm deepened. A nod in the morning. A glance when a child ran past the shop window, laughing. She began listening for the sound of his shoes on the alley stones. Once, he placed a small orange blossom on her table without saying a word. She let it stay, wilting in the warmth throughout the day.

It wasn't love. Not yet. It was something slower.

In time, their hands met again, not by accident. His fingers brushed hers as he helped fold fabric, and this time, they lingered—tentative but certain. Two people learning a language built from quiet.

One golden evening, she offered him a corner of her scarf to hold as she stitched.

"If you're going to sit there," she said lightly, "you might as well be useful."

He smiled—that quiet, shy smile she was beginning to memorize.

Later, as the bells from the church tower tolled vespers, Ana began humming under her breath—a Jewish lullaby, half—remembered. David listened and then softly joined her.

Their voices wove together—not perfectly, but sincerely: "Oyfn pripetshik brent a fayerl..."

It wasn't only for Roza. It was for what might still be saved. For what still lived inside them.

David reached into his pocket and drew out a small woven bracelet, blue thread embroidered with a Star of David. "From my mother," he said. "She gave it to me when I turned thirteen. I think she would have liked you."

He didn't place it on her wrist. He only offered it, and Ana took it with both hands, bowing her head.

The day he didn't come, she realized how much she had come to expect his presence. But the next morning, he returned—carrying two cannolis and a small paper bag with sugared almonds.

"I thought," he said, almost shyly, "we might sit outside today."

Ana glanced at the light warming the stones of the piazza. A child's laughter rang from somewhere unseen. She nodded.

They stepped into the light together. Not healed. Not whole. But together.

Chapter Twenty-Four
Beginning

The synagogue was modest—tucked between sun—warmed stone walls on a quiet Florentian street. Its wooden benches creaked softly, and sunlight spilled through narrow windows in golden shafts that danced on the tiled floor. There was no choir, no grandeur, only a hush—reverent and real.

Ana stood beneath the chuppah, stitched with linen she had dyed and sewn herself. Each thread held a memory, woven with quiet grief and the stubborn will to begin again. The canopy fluttered slightly in the breeze that slipped through a half—open door, like the breath of something ancient—something still alive.

David stood beside her. His tallit rested over his shoulders, and his dark wool suit fit him with quiet dignity. He had been a man of fabric—a merchant who touched silks and cottons the way others touched lives: carefully, deliberately. Now, he was a man holding onto what threads remained.

The rabbi, old and soft-spoken, murmured blessings in Hebrew. The sound of it pulled at something deep in Ana's chest—not memory, exactly, but recognition. A belonging that refused to be erased. But even here, even now, her mind wandered.

She remembered her first wedding—a town hall barely lit and cold with the whispers of wartime vows. Vasyl had held her hand so tightly, as if he could stop time. A simple headscarf and the promise of the future together, while the horizon had already burned.

And David, too, was elsewhere for a moment. Malka had worn a white dress when they married. No lace, but bright. Clean. Her hair was braided with tiny silver pins. They were happy. Not yet, parents. Not yet hunted. Just two people who still believed in beginnings. But her name had vanished in smoke.

Ana had known Malka later—not as a bride, but as a woman bent by hunger, softened by sorrow. In the barracks, Malka had been the one who gave Ana a cloth when no one else had anything. The one who held Ana's hand as blood soaked the straw. The one who said nothing, but whose silence spoke of endurance.

And now, here. Florence. Under a cloth canopy instead of a gray sky, Ana took David's hand. His fingers trembled, older than hers, but steady.

She whispered, "There is no music. But I still hear the humming."

David looked down. "I do too."

The rabbi offered them wine—deep red, like memory. They drank.

And when the time came, David crushed the glass beneath his foot. The sharp crack echoed in the quiet synagogue like a final chapter closing.

For a moment, neither of them moved. Then, hand in hand, they stepped into the Florentine afternoon. The sky hung low, the air sweet with rain. The city watched silently as two strangers, stitched together by war and loss, walked forward.

"We've both buried weddings," David said softly.

Ana nodded. "But this one… this one is made by our own hands."

He smiled gently. "We'll make something lasting."

"And soft," she added, almost laughing. "Not like the world we came from."

Together, they walked down the narrow cobbled street, past shuttered windows and the scent of rising bread.

Not untouched. Not unbroken. But still here. Now—beginning.

Chapter Twenty-Five
Across

The ship pulled away from Florence under a pale morning sky, its hull slicing through the calm waters of the Mediterranean like a tired heartbeat. It wasn't a grand vessel, a transport refitted to carry the displaced—the broken, the rebuilt, the nameless souls seeking land beneath their feet and air that didn't carry the stench of smoke and silence.

Ana stood at the railing, her hand tightening on the coarse metal. The salt of the sea clung to her lips, and her eyes watered from the wind—though it could have been something else. Behind her, Italy receded like a dream she no longer believed in. Before her, America waited—a word more than a place, wrapped in myth and imagined kindness.

David appeared beside her, quiet as always, with his scarf in his hand. He didn't ask. He simply draped it across her shoulders and stood beside her, his presence calm and grounded.

She glanced at him—not the way she used to look at men in the years before war, but with the eyes of someone who had learned what it meant to rebuild a world with nothing but fragments and fabric.

All around them, life stirred. A young couple stood farther down the deck, fingers intertwined, their belongings wrapped in cloth bundles at their feet. The woman was visibly pregnant, and when she laughed, it was the sound of something daring to return. A boy no older than ten darted past them, chasing a bit of string like it was a kite. His shoes didn't match, but his grin did not falter. An old man nearby played a mouth organ softly, the melody clumsy but joyful.

Not everyone spoke. Not everyone smiled. But in pockets and corners, hope emerged—like weeds pushing through cracked concrete. These were people touched by the same grief Ana carried in her bones. Yet somehow, some of them still believed in the promise of a morning without shadows.

The days blurred into one another. The food was plain. People kept to themselves or spoke in soft tongues-Russian, Ukrainian, Yiddish, German, Polish, and Italian. Languages once used to pray, love, and cry out for family were now reduced to whispers of survival.

At night, Ana would lie on the narrow bunk beneath the flickering overhead lamp and listen to David's breath slow beside her. She didn't sleep much, but when she did, she dreamt in fabric—colours folding, torn threads being mended, patterns emerging out of nothing.

Once, as the ship swayed gently and the stars blinked into the ink sky, she whispered, "Will we be enough?"

David didn't answer immediately.

Then, in a voice as soft as cloth being folded, he said, "We're alive. That's already more than we were."

She didn't need more than that.

Early in the morning, she went above deck and looked out toward the empty sea. The wind braided through her hair. Somewhere behind her, there were ashes. Camps. Chimneys. Graves marked with crosses and names she rarely said aloud. But ahead—somewhere far but certain—was a life she had not chosen, but one she would now begin.

The ship groaned forward, carrying its living cargo westward.-a floating orphanage of memory and hope. Ana reached into her coat and touched a folded square of linen.

The last thing she embroidered before leaving Italy. A rose. Not blooming yet, just beginning to open. Roza. She held it close. No one noticed the way her thumb moved gently over the stitches. It was a habit. It was a prayer. Ana knew when the land would come into view, days later—a hazy line breaking the horizon-Ana wouldn't weep.

She stood taller. There was no returning to who she was. There was only the life still ahead—uncertain, unfinished. But hers.

Chapter Twenty-Six
Touch

The deck was nearly empty. Just the hush of waves, the smell of salt and iron, and the stars—scattered across the sky like prayers that had burnt through. Below, someone played a soft, lilting tune on an accordion—uneven, worn at the edges, like memory. A child's lullaby turned inside out.

Ana stood near the railing, arms folded against the cold. The sea shimmered under moonlight, and something in her—the part that still remembered music and kitchens and dancing barefoot in summer—stirred.

David approached, his coat unbuttoned, scarf tugged loose. He didn't speak.

She turned to him. "Dance with me."

He blinked. "Here?"

She nodded. "Why not?"

He offered his hand. She didn't hesitate. They stepped close, barely touching—their bodies swaying with the ship's rhythm. At first, it was awkward.-a shuffled balance between waves and breath. But then, something softened.

Her hand slipped to his shoulder, his to her waist, and they began to move in slow, circling steps. His palm was warm through her blouse. She felt the strength of his hand, but also its gentleness—the way it held without claiming.

They didn't speak. She let her cheek rest near his collarbone, her breath catching at the way their bodies aligned. Not perfectly. But honestly. The scent of him—warm wool, skin, the faintest trace of soap—rose around her.

And the shape of him, solid and near, awakened something that wasn't fear. It was want. Not hunger. Not need. Want. For a touch.

He moved with her as though he'd always known this tempo. His fingers tightened slightly on her waist when the ship tilted. Her body answered without thinking, pressing closer. She felt the heat rise between them—not sharp, not sudden, but blooming. Slow. Like something remembered after too long in the dark.

She lifted her face to his. Their eyes met. She smiled shyly. And so did he. The space between them changed, twisted in single threads into one rope.

And softly, deliberately, she whispered, "Come."

They moved through the ship's narrow corridors without speaking. The hush between them had changed—no longer the silence of grief, but of breath held in wonder. Her hand brushed his as they climbed the narrow stairs. This time, she didn't pull away.

The door to their small cabin creaked shut behind them. He hesitated by the bed—the thin mattress, the blanket barely more than cloth. It wasn't much. But she had known far less.

Ana untied the scarf from her shoulders. Folded it neatly. Set it down on the dresser. Then she turned to him and reached for the buttons of his shirt—slow, deliberate. Not shy. Not bold. Just sure. Her fingers trembled once—and she laughed, the sound quiet and surprised.

David looked at her, startled, then smiled—that same boyish, uneven smile that had slipped out once or twice in the tailor shop.

"Was that your first laugh in months?" he asked.

She grinned. "Maybe years."

He raised his arms slightly, mock—formal. "Well then. Shall I stand very still while you undress me, or…?"

She rolled her eyes and touched his chest, feeling the rising heartbeat. "Don't ruin it."

But there was laughter between them now, quiet and warm, stitched into the seams of their closeness.

His voice whispered. "Are you sure?"

"I am," she said, looking at him without blinking.

He stilled—not because he doubted her, but because of the reverence in her voice. He nodded, then reached for her blouse, his fingers catching on a button.

"Stubborn little thing," he muttered.

She smirked. "That one's always been difficult."

They both laughed—not loud, not careless, but real. The ship shifted beneath them, groaning slightly, as if in approval.

When her blouse fell away, and then his shirt, she looked at his bare shoulders and said, teasing, "Not bad for a man who claims to be too old for dancing."

He flushed, touched her cheek. "You make me feel… younger than I am. Like something is still beginning."

They lay down together, close but not urgent. Their bodies met like the tide meeting shore—hesitant, then sure. Her hand explored the shape of his shoulder, his ribs, his breath. His touch lingered on her back, her hip, the hollow of her arm. She giggled once when his thumb grazed a ticklish spot near her ribs, and he looked mortified.

"I didn't mean to-"

She kissed him lightly to quiet the apology. "I didn't say stop."

His hand slowly touched the numbers on her hand, and she did not flinch. The numbers no longer felt as a mark of death but rather the ink of pain endured, but no longer acute.

Later, when the laughter stilled and their limbs softened into quiet, Ana rested her head beneath his chin. The lantern above swayed gently, casting quiet shadows on the walls. There was no urgency as the time stood still. No proving. Only two people who were laying down their grief and reaching for something gentle.

"I've not felt…" she began, but didn't finish.

"You don't have to," he said.

Outside, the sea kept whispering. Inside, they breathed—together, quiet and alive. The ship moved beneath them, old wood rocking in a rhythm as old as the world. She closed her eyes, still smiling.

David whispered, "You are not alone."

"I know," she said.

And she meant it. And something inside her—a thread long frayed—held.

Chapter Twenty-Seven
Landed

The building was tall and brownstone, creaking slightly with age. On the third floor, in a modest apartment filled with the smell of boiled coffee and warm dust, Ana opened a window and let in the city. New York. It roared outside—trolley bells, impatient horns, and the hum of languages layered over each other like patchwork quilts. In the distance, children shouted in English, their laughter skipping like stones across the tenement walls.

Ana didn't mind the noise. After silence, even chaos could be comforting. She no longer minded the sounds that brought back a faint memory of Roza—but she still felt the thread that connected them as an invisible umbilical cord.

Inside, she had created a quiet world of her own. A long table was pressed against the wall, a rack of spools was stacked in a careful gradient, and squares of silk and linen she had brought from Italy were folded neatly atop the wooden surface—fabric with memory stitched into every thread. She worked with her sleeves rolled up, her needle moving in precise rhythm. Rose petals. Four stages of life. Always the fleeting, lively, beautiful rose flower in the center.

Downstairs, Mrs. Mayflower, the neighbour, had once caught sight of Ana as she left for the market, arm in arm with David. Ana remembered the glance—sharp, assessing, with a half—smile laced with pity.

Later, she overheard the old hack whispering to another neighbour in the stairwell, "He should still be grieving his wife. And now—this one, with her accent and so young. A widower's heart can get confused, tempted."

Ana didn't flinch when she heard it. Instead, she went upstairs, closed the door, and picked up her embroidery again. A single red thread pulled through white silk, the first stroke of a new petal.

David never said anything about the whispers. He had heard them too—in the shop, at synagogue. But he didn't answer to them.

He came home every evening with a cannoli wrapped in a brown bag and placed it on the counter with a quiet, "Thought you might be hungry."

Some days, they talked, and some days, they simply sat, two people with pasts too heavy to carry aloud. But the silence was not empty between them—it breathed, mended, and held space.

One day, Ana finished another scarf—a blooming rose in the center, and Roza in the four corners, at every age she might have been. She didn't name the figure, didn't explain the signs—the grieving mother's mark in the corner, a hand with a broken heart and a single blue tear. She folded it carefully and placed it on the top shelf with the almost identical first scarf that brought them together.

That night, David found her humming a lullaby, sewing by the window, her back to the door. He didn't speak, just stood for a moment, watching the red petals bloom under her needle on the new silk square.

And for the first time, he said, "I would have liked to meet your daughter."

Ana's hand paused.

She looked up at him and nodded once. "She would have liked you," she said.

"And my girls", David paused, "they all could've…" and he stopped as if his voice suddenly became a thread abruptly cut with the scissors.

The city buzzed around them, lights blinking across rooftops, traffic rolling down Fifth Avenue like a restless tide.

And in their apartment, the scent of thread, silk, and memory rose softly—not grief, not yet healing—but something like hope, stitched one rose at a time.

Chapter Twenty-Eight
Numbered

They called it a close-knit community. They donated faithfully, tucking money into small envelopes and stitching it into the seams of the synagogue like contrition. The names of the dead were engraved on plaques and hung in tidy rows—gold letters for those who perished in the smoke. There were no photos or stories—just the names—clean, quiet, safely mounted on the wood.

They gathered on Shabbat: white tablecloths, braided bread, candlesticks lit with reverence and resignation, a hush over everything. The children were quiet. The elders were quieter still. Laughter, when it came, felt rehearsed. Sometimes, there was music, but never dancing.

The men wore wool suits and shook hands with the gravity of accountants. The women passed kugel and compliments across polished tables, their lipstick precisely drawn. Grief tucked into pearls and good posture.

They asked Ana where she was from—not out of cruelty, but out of structure. That question was allowed. Where, not what, not how, never who was lost.

She answered simply: "Europe."

They nodded, as if that explained the accent, the silences, the eyes.

David sat beside her, his hands carefully placed in his lap. He did not speak for her—he never did. But he noticed the way her shoulders stiffened at the question, the way her eyes retreated inward, and the soft click of a door closing behind them.

They were kind to him, too—kinder, perhaps. He was one of theirs. Born there but came here before the fire. But touched by it. In the most unimaginable way. They asked about his factory, his trips to Italy, and whether he planned to remarry. He answered with enough warmth to be polite.

And then he brought Ana—the one with the numbers on her arm.

Their Shabbat dinners were a lonely, tightly held family tradition, familiar to both, but without children at the table, it felt like a chore. They still lit the candles and said prayers, but never touched the topic of the children. Not because they couldn't speak of the children lost but because they knew that they couldn't bring the new ones into the world, not by choice but by man's doing. And so the quiet filled their Shabbat dinners, but it was enough.

The Katz family was the only one brave enough to invite them to their Shabbat, not out of pity but out of human charity.

The Shabbat dinner was held in a tall house with a narrow staircase and a kitchen that smelled of onions and bleach. The hostess wore a silk blouse and diamond studs. She touched Ana's wrist as she passed the challah, as if uncertain she was real.

There were twelve people at the table. Four children. No noise.

They sang the blessings softly, without harmony. Ana watched the candles flicker in the window's reflection. She did not know the tunes—not these versions, not this language. She whispered the old melodies under her breath, the ones from before—in Yiddish, in Ukrainian, in the hush of women who no longer had mouths.

David glanced at her. Not asking, not intruding—just there.

They ate brisket and tzimmes, spooned kugel from a floral dish. Someone made a joke about gefilte fish and American refrigerators. Someone else mentioned Israel.

No one asked about Poland, Ukraine or Russia. Or ashes. Or where their daughters were buried. No one spoke of trains. No one spoke of numbered hands or stripes. Stripes were acceptable in the zoo.

Ana smiled softly when it was required. She said thank you quietly. She gently passed the dishes. She kept her eyes low. But she felt her silence like heat rising beneath her dress. Her grief sat beside her, uninvited but not unnoticed.

They were the ones who had stayed. Or left in time. Their sorrow had an architecture. A budget. A plaque. They mourned safely, in English.

Ana was not angry with them. She did not expect them to know.

But when they said "never again," they meant never to us. Never in Brooklyn, Manhattan or even Jersey. Never in this language. Never where anyone might smell the smoke. Touch the ashes.

She shared their faith, their holidays, and their songs. But now it felt like playing music underwater. They were made of the same cloth, but they had been cut differently. Some of them were counted, and some of them were burnt.

Chapter Twenty-Nine
Boiled

The kettle hissed softly in the background. Not screaming yet, just breathing steam. Ana moved through the apartment like a current, her steps light but relentless, like her mother had on Fridays before the war, when even the spoons gleamed with ritual.

All day, the apartment filled with the scent of cinnamon and onions, of yeast rising and beets cooling on the windowsill. She braided the challah three times before deciding it wasn't right and starting again. She pressed lace over the table, polished the candlesticks, and set out canolis on a plate that no one would notice but her. Two wine glasses. Six more. The room waited with its breath held.

David came in once to ask if she needed help, but Ana only shook her head. She was holding herself together like a thread in a seam—one tug and she'd come undone.

By six, everything glowed. The table shimmered under the low light, bowls nested, steam lifting from the pot on the stove. She'd never hosted a full Shabbat before—not in New York, not ever. But she had invited them. She had tried. Her new community. She had spoken clearly.

She had said, "Come!"

Now it was seven. Then eight. The soup boiled down.

David stood leaning against the doorframe. "Maybe they forgot. Or something came up," he said gently.

Ana stared at the table. "Something came up for all of them?"

He didn't answer. The air thickened. The kettle began to rattle faintly on the back burner.

Ana didn't look at him when she spoke: "I tried. And they dissed me. They smiled when I spoke to them in the synagogue and nodded. They said it would be nice. They lied!"

David blinked. "What?"

"I tried," she said louder now, the words rising like the water in the pot, "I opened my house. I invited them in. I cooked everything, and they didn't even say 'no". They just didn't come."

"It's not personal, Ana."

"Don't 'Ana' me like that. Don't-"

Her fist slammed the table. The candlesticks rattled. The wine spilled in a red arc across the cloth like a wound.

"I cooked all day. I invited everyone. I made a place for them. What else do they want from me?" Her voice was becoming louder, "I boil myself down to nothing, and still I'm tired of trying to be someone they might like. I am not from here, David. I will never be from here. But I still hoped-"

"And that hope is what I love about you."

But her back was turned. She stood rigid in the kitchen, jaw clenched, her chest rising and falling like she'd run through fire.

"They don't have to say "yes". That's what you don't get. Not saying anything. It's worse. It's like I don't even exist."

He stepped toward her: "You do exist. You exist to me."

"Oh, that's very generous," she snapped, her voice curving sharply, "I guess I should be grateful I have one person."

David recoiled, stunned.

And then she broke—not tears yet, but volume: "Do you know what it is like to be invisible in the place where you're trying so hard to belong? To build something again, even a Friday, even a table, even a potato salad? And then have no one come? Do you!?"

David opened his mouth, then closed it: "I do know something about being invisible," he said finally, voice tight, "But this isn't about me, is it?"

"No," she said, suddenly tired. "No, it isn't."

The kettle shrieked behind them. She yanked it from the stove and spilled water on the floor. Her hands were shaking.

David stepped forward, slow, uncertain. "It doesn't mean you're not wanted."

But she was sobbing now, full—bodied, sharp with rage. "Then where are they? Why do I set a table for ghosts?"

He didn't answer. They stood in mounting silence.

Then—a knock.

David startled and turned. Ana didn't move.

Another knock.

David walked to the door and opened it. Ana turned and stepped to it.

On the threshold stood Mrs. Mayflower, about eighty years old and not a day older, dressed in a floral coat with two brooches on each side and a hat the colour of an old rose. Her pink lipstick had feathered past the lip line. Her green eyes were keen, unbothered.

"I heard shouting," she said, peering past Ana into the apartment. "Thought someone was being killed."

Ana couldn't speak. Her face froze. A dozen thoughts passed through like ghosts—how Mrs. Mayflower would twist this into gossip, how she'd tell the neighbours about the foreign woman with the full table, empty chairs, and spilled wine.

Mrs. Mayflower's eyes moved past David, landing on the table set for eight, glinting with absence.

She hesitated, then took a step in: "Did I miss the crowd?"

"There isn't one," Ana said flatly.

"Shame," said Mrs. Mayflower.

Then she entered like it was her right, and maybe it was.

"Well," she said, removing her coat. "We'll just pretend I was invited."

The room held its breath.

David nodded, grabbed her coat and put it on the coat rack, then went inside and pulled out a chair: "Please."

Mrs. Mayflower sat and filled the spot as if she were the matriarch of the family. Her flowery dress bloomed in the room.

Ana blinked. Then moved to the table. Slowly.

David pulled out a chair for Ana, but she didn't move. Not at first.

Not until Mrs. Mayflower took a long look at the table—the platters untouched, the glasses clear—and said, "When the new came, and the old started packing up and leaving—I stayed. I don't care where people are from. Good or bad is all I see. And the new ones?" She paused, meeting Ana's eyes. "You aren't either. Yet."

Ana lowered herself into the chair.

The silence cracked a little, like a crust on a cooling loaf.

David, the last man standing, sat too.

"My son loved potato salad. Used to eat it cold out of the fridge before the deployment," Mrs. Mayflower said. "Before the war. He was a naval officer. Pacific. His name was James."

She said the name like a ritual, as if it still echoed on ships and under waves.

"He died?" Ana asked quietly.

"1944. Never found the body. I don't talk about it often. But tonight feels like it matters."

Ana nodded slowly. "Vasyl was in the Red Army. Killed in the first months of the war. Our war, Soviet Union war."

Mrs. Mayflower nodded and pointed to the candles, "Should we?"

They lit the candles. The shadows on the walls appeared as more guests walked in.

Then Mrs. Mayflower crossed herself as a matter of fact. "In the name of the Father, the Son, and the Holy Spirit."

Ana whispered, "Baruch atah Adonai, Eloheinu Melech ha'olam, asher kid'shanu b'mitzvotav…"

And so two women, ripped by loss and stitched by time passed, sat across a lace—covered table, praying different prayers, over the same flame.

David remained silent, as if the ritual happening in front of his eyes was something that this Shabbat needed and that God approved of. The three of them were no longer strangers but survivors. And the table no longer glimmered—it breathed.

Outside, the city spun on. Inside, threads of invisible kindness bound them—soft, improvised, real—not a tapestry, not yet.

For a moment, the chairs did not feel empty. They felt filled—not with the past lost but with the past that happened. Vasyl, Roza, Halyna, Malka, Rivka, Tova, Miriam, Ana's parents, David's parents, and James. The family was there, in the glimmer of the candlelight, in the steam rising from the food, in the soft hush of breath between strangers.

And Ana-Ana did not feel alone anymore.

Chapter Thirty
Building

It started slowly, like moss growing between the cracks. After the silence. After the storm. Ana began walking again. Just the streets at first-Avenue J to the park, the bakery, the corner where the girls sold bobby pins and laughter. She kept her head down, but she didn't hide. Some women nodded. One even said good morning.

She started bringing tea to synagogue potlucks, never staying long. When she left, the cups were always empty. Sometimes there was a thank—you note on the tray, and sometimes there was not.

She learned names. She forgot others. She made a list, quietly, in the back of her drawer:

Liba—daughter with long sleeves.

Mrs. Hirsch—pink glasses.

Little Ruth—broken tooth.

Miriam—soft voice, fierce eyes.

She didn't try too hard. Not anymore. The kettle had boiled. Now came the slow simmer. The days repeated. Streets, stitches, Shabbat. Names learned, names forgotten. It was not dramatic, not even remarkable. It was simply the slow, humble work of living.

She volunteered to mend things—hems, broken buttons, a stuffed bear's ear. She left her name off the parcels but began stitching a tiny thread mark at each hem: a small n, as in Nityak. Threader.

David called her "The Quiet Seamstress of the East End," and she smiled in a way that softened the years between them.

Children waved. A boy with a missing shoelace followed her once and asked what she was humming.

"Nothing," she said.

But it was a lullaby, the one that her mother used to sing in the old apartment above the shop. She sang it again, once, at dusk, under her breath as the laundry flapped like doves on the line.

David brought home news from the factory floor—someone's cousin liked the apple pie, someone else said her embroidery reminded them of Kraków. A woman named Chava asked for help with a wedding shawl. Ana did not flinch.

The people who hadn't come that night never spoke of it.

But one woman, older than Mrs. Mayflower, pressed a wrapped parcel into her hands one morning: boiled potatoes, eggs, and onions. "For Shabbat," she said. "No one should eat alone."

She ate with David. They lit the candles. They blessed the bread. Some nights, they laughed. Some nights they didn't. The grief didn't vanish—it wove itself in, like a coarse thread in linen. But she was no longer only pulling.

In the spring, they asked if she would teach a sewing class for girls, mothers, and anyone who wanted to make something whole again. She said yes. She wore her bracelet, the one that David gave her in Italy. She carried her thimble. She passed Mrs. Mayflower's window, where geraniums bloomed with stubborn joy.

Then David asked Ana to help at the factory, and she agreed to be there, first once a week, then twice, then every day. She passed the window and waved to Mrs. Mayflower every morning on the way to work.

Then, one day, the window was empty—the chair and the lace were gone, and the air was still.

But Ana knew that when God came for Mrs. Mayflower, she wasn't alone. There was light in her apartment. A bowl of freshly made potato salad was still in the fridge. And, Ana liked to believe, the invisible threads—all the human kindnesses she had ever given—were winding their way home.

Once, on a quiet evening, Ana set the table again: two plates, two cups, and no guests.

Just them. And that day, it felt as if she was finally home.

Chapter Thirty-One
Rip

The scarves began as simple pieces of fabric, delicate as whispers. But in Ana's hands, they became stories—woven threads of memory, loss, and hope. Each scarf bore the mark of her past, hidden beneath patterns and colours: Roza's scar, the fragile bloom of a rose, the four faces of life—child, youth, adulthood, and old age. Collectors and connoisseurs felt the weight behind these works. They were not just fashion; they were fragile vessels of survival, worn or hung as art.

David's factory hummed with renewed purpose. Under Ana's careful management, the once modest textile business grew, blending tradition with modern craft. She handled logistics and design decisions with quiet competence, her sharp eye catching details others missed. David, with his gentle authority and soft smiles, stood beside her—a partner in rebuilding the shards of their shattered worlds.

They moved into an apartment on Fifth Avenue, the kind of place their old selves could only dream of. The building was elegant but never ostentatious, much like them. Light filtered through tall windows, touching the worn wood floors and the simple, tasteful furniture Ana carefully chose. The walls held little decoration—just a few paintings and the embroidered scarves framed in quiet homage.

Neighbours in the building were quick to whisper. To some, Ana was the trophy wife—a stranger with a dark past and a wealthy husband. But those whispers bounced off her like dust in the sunlight. Ana and David had no illusions about their lives. They were not people who sought excess or flash. They had known hunger, fear, and loss. Humility and gratitude had settled deep into their bones.

As time passed, David grew tired more quickly than he used to. He'd pause halfway up the stairs, pressing one hand to the rail and the other to his chest, just for a breath. His doctor called it nothing urgent-"just the heart reminding you it's been working a long time."

Ana noticed the change in his gait, the way he leaned against the kitchen counter a moment longer than necessary. Quietly, she began placing his pills beside his morning tea, watching his plate more than her own. It was unspoken between them, but gently understood: if illness came, it would come for him first. He was older. He had lived the years before she was even born. But fate, as ever, had its own sharp edge.

One late Sunday afternoon, as Ana worked on a new scarf pattern, David came in from the window, setting down a cup of tea beside her.

"You've been at it all day," he said gently, watching her threading the delicate rose unfolding under her needle.

Ana looked up, a tired smile touching her lips. "This one… It's different. I want it to feel like… new life. Fragile but strong."

David nodded, squeezing her hand. "Just like you."

She laughed softly. "Don't make me cry, or I'll ruin the silk."

He grinned. "I'd never do that. Though… maybe a tear would make it more real."

The room was filled with quiet warmth.

But as night fell, Ana suddenly clutched her stomach. She bent over the edge of the table, then rushed to the small bathroom.

David's voice was urgent but calm. "Ana? What's wrong?"

She barely whispered, "I don't know…"

The sound of retching echoed softly as the lights flickered.

David's face paled, caught between fear and helplessness.

Outside, the city lights twinkled, unaware of the fragile life inside this quiet apartment, and a new storm was about to unfold.

Chapter Thirty-Two
Breath

The harsh fluorescent lights buzzed overhead as Ana lay on the narrow hospital bed, her skin pale and clammy. The relentless nausea had drained her strength, and the growing heaviness in her belly was impossible to ignore. Vomiting had become almost daily, each episode stealing more of her energy—but no one could explain why.

David sat beside her, worry etched deeply into his face. His fingers nervously twisted a corner of her bedsheet. The sterile scent of antiseptic filled the air, sharp and unforgiving.

"Ana, what's happening to you?" he asked quietly, voice thick with fear. "You're so weak… and this —it doesn't make sense."

She tried to smile, but it faltered, the dry taste of sickness clinging to her mouth. "I don't know, David. The doctors… they're worried."

A nurse entered briskly, clipboard in hand. "They want to keep you for observation a bit longer," she said gently, avoiding Ana's eyes.

David gripped Ana's hand tighter, his knuckles white.

"Is it… cancer?" he whispered, dread creeping in, "is she…"

Ana closed her eyes, heart pounding. The thought had crossed her mind—the weight of all she had survived now threatened by an invisible threat inside her own body. Her life will end soon. She made it this far only to die from this impossible—to—diagnose illness.

Doctors came and went, murmuring in hushed tones, running tests and taking notes. The days passed slowly, Ana's hope dimming with each weary breath.

Then one morning, the lead doctor appeared, his face unreadable.

"Ana," he said quietly, "we don't have the full explanation yet, but your condition… It's different."

David leaned forward. "Different how?"

The doctor hesitated, then said, "You're… expecting."

"Expecting what?" Ana asked, bracing for a diagnosis. Her mind filled in: a disease, a tumour,-all a death sentence.

David blinked and laughed—the sound small, disbelieving. "A baby?"

Ana stared at him. "A baby? After everything? I am not dying?"

The doctor nodded. "It's rare, but it explains the symptoms. The sickness, the swelling. We'll continue monitoring, but it's clear. And, no, you are not dying. Just quite the opposite."

David leaned forward and kissed her forehead. "We'll go through this. Together."

As the doctor left, Ana lay back, tears wetting the corners of her eyes. Wonder bloomed inside her like a slow, stubborn seed.

And then, softly, from some deep place within her, she began to hum.

It wasn't conscious. It was the instinct. A lullaby long buried—once sung in Yiddish, once in Ukrainian—drifted up from the roots of memory. She whispered the words under her breath, and the tune—passed down by women who no longer had mouths, who lived only in the hush between heartbeats—slowly spread the news: life did not die, the child would be born, and the thread would go on weaving.

"Oyfn pripetshik brent a fayerl..." Then, more quietly: "Spi, moye dytya..."-sleep, my child...

It was not only for their unborn child that Ana already loved. It was for Roza, for Rivka, Toba, and Miriam. For all the girls she could not cradle, all the children, wanted or unwanted, she lost, held, or imagined.

The lullaby was a thread, stitching time to time, womb to grave, silence to sound.

David sat quietly, listening. And Ana sang on. Her voice was weak but steady, a fragile thread of hope weaving through the sterile hospital room that bloomed with life this time, not death.

Chapter Thirty-Three
Unbroken

Ana lay still in the hospital bed, her body fragile like delicate porcelain—a vase barely holding together under the weight of upcoming storms. Each breath was measured, each movement careful not to crack the surface of her being.

David sat nearby, hands clenched, eyes shadowed by a conflict he dared not voice aloud. He loved the tiny life growing inside her—a miracle after so much loss—but with that love came a gnawing guilt.

He remembered the years of pain they'd both endured, the shadows of those who never returned. He wanted this child with all his heart, yet a whisper of selfishness haunted him.

"How can I want this happiness," he thought, "when it reminds me of all the lives lost? When it makes me feel like I'm betraying those ghosts?"

He reached out, brushing a stray lock of hair from Ana's forehead, careful not to disturb her rest. She opened her eyes, meeting him with a faint, weary smile—a silent acknowledgment of the fragile hope between them.

David whispered, "We'll protect this life, Ana. No matter what."

Ana's fingers closed weakly around his hand—like the vase she was, holding within her a new beginning. The thought of wanting this child more than anything in the world wrapped her mind. She did not feel as if she betrayed her dead children but as if God had given her one last chance to produce life and care for that life.

And then inside, Ana's thoughts churned like water under ice. She felt suspended between terror and wonder, her body no longer only her own but a vessel for something she both longed for and feared. The child inside her was hope made flesh—but also a reminder of how easily life could be taken, how fragile even the strongest thread could be.

Her hand on David's felt like an anchor, but also a question: would he still hold on if she faltered, if her body betrayed her? She thought of the women she had known—mothers who had lost children, wives who had buried husbands—and wondered if she was destined to join their ranks, destined to carry grief as her inheritance, not a baby.

Still, beneath the fear, there was a small flame—a stubborn pulse of defiance. She wanted this life, even if it broke her. She wanted to believe that something could be stitched whole again after so much unravelling.

Her eyes fluttered shut, but her heart whispered silently: "Let me be a mother, again. Let me keep this child. Let me learn how to live, not just survive. Let me see him grow. God, you owe me this one, for all the ones you have taken."

She smiled as she felt a little kick inside, as if the baby acknowledged that he would be here soon. She cradled her belly under the white hospital sheets, and after many uncertain days, she fell asleep peacefully.

And with David's hand wrapped around hers, they were no longer two broken people but a family.

Chapter Thirty-Four
New

The hospital room was hushed, the heavy quiet broken only by Ana's slow, laboured breaths and the soft ticking of the clock on the wall. Outside, the city hummed in an indifferent rhythm, but inside this small space, time seemed to stretch, suspended between fear and hope. David begged to stay, and the Doctor friend allowed him.

David sat close, his hand wrapped tightly around Ana's. His palm was slick with sweat, but his grip never wavered. His heart thundered in his chest, a relentless drum that echoed every moment, every contraction.

Ana's face was pale and drawn, but her eyes held a flicker of fierce determination. "Almost there," the nurse whispered, her voice calm and steady, a tether in the storm.

Then, suddenly—a sharp, piercing cry cut through the room.

A sound so fragile and yet so alive, it stopped David's breath.

The baby's tiny body was carefully lifted and placed in Ana's arms, warm against her skin, a fragile weight that held the promise of all that was to come. His fists curled instinctively, his little chest rising and falling like a whispered prayer.

Tears welled in Ana's eyes, a mix of relief, exhaustion, and overwhelming love. She looked down at him—this small miracle born out of pain and sacrifice.

David leaned closer, voice barely above a whisper but trembling with emotion. "He's ours."

They sat together, silent for a moment, the new life between them the axis on which their world now turned.

Choosing a name felt like carving a future out of the past.

"Eli," David said softly, "My grandfather's name. It means 'ascended'-rising, reaching upward."

Ana's lips curved in a tired, hopeful smile. "Yes… Eli. A new beginning."

The baby stirred, a tiny sigh escaping him as if answering their silent vow.

In that small room, amid the shadows of all they had lost, a fragile hope bloomed—fierce and unyielding as the love that would hold him safe. Outside, the city continued on, unaware of the quiet miracle unfolding within. But for Ana and David, nothing would ever be the same again.

The peace did not last.

Moments after the nurse carried Eli into the station, a red bloom spread beneath Ana, soaking through the fresh sheets. The room shifted in an instant—the steady hum of the hospital became sharp and frantic. Hands pressed against her abdomen, voices rose in clipped commands.

David froze, his body stone and fire all at once. He had seen blood before, too much of it, but never hers—never like this.

"Stay outside," someone ordered, and before he could answer, they were taking her away, the wheels of the bed rattling against the floor like a drumbeat of dread. The last glimpse he caught was her pale face, eyes shut, lips parted as if whispering a prayer she had no breath to finish.

The doors swung closed. The window between them was suddenly blank, and David was left holding nothing. He turned back and walked to the nursery, where Eli lay swaddled in impossibly white cloth with the two rows of other newborns. His son's chest rose and fell, steady and defiant. David rose and followed, his eyes pressed to the glass, afraid to blink, as though sight alone tethered his son to this world.

It was there, in that sliver of a view, that something shifted. He saw more than a newborn behind the pane. He saw a boy with skinned knees chasing after a ball, his laughter high and certain. He saw a teenager, tall and restless, shoulders too narrow for the weight he would one day bear. He saw an older man with a familiar and strange face—a face that had his eyes but Ana's stubborn jaw. A man who stood in the light of a future David could barely imagine, and yet believed in with his whole being.

The visions came like flashes, like photographs tucked one after another into his mind. For the first time since the war, he saw a thread stretching forward, not back—not only ghosts but beginnings.

He pressed his palm against the cool glass, whispering so softly it was only for himself: "You will live, my son. You will carry us forward."

David pressed his forehead against the glass, tears sliding freely now. He begged silently, fiercely, for Ana's life.

Hours later, when the doors finally opened, the doctor stepped out with weary eyes. "She's alive," he said, "but the bleeding was severe. We had to remove her uterus. She will not bear more children."

The words cut and soothed all at once. Relief and grief collided inside David's chest, leaving him shaking.

When at last he was allowed back in, Ana was pale but breathing, her body diminished yet still here. He sat at her side, taking her hand in both of his. He would not tell her yet, not tonight, that Eli was her last. For now, all that mattered was that the thread of her life had held.

He glanced again toward the window where their son slept and whispered into the fragile silence: "This one child will be enough. He will be ours forever."

When she finally woke, weak and hollowed out, Ana understood without being told. The ache inside her was not just from the incision but from an emptiness deeper than flesh. She would never carry another child.

And yet, when her eyes found Eli sleeping in David's arms, her heart did not break. Instead, it steadied. She felt, with a clarity that surprised her, that this was the price she had agreed to in her prayers, though she had not spoken it aloud. God had taken her womb, but He had given her this boy. It was a bargain she could live with.

She whispered, "Then let it be so. One life, one future. We will pour everything into him."

There was no bitterness in her voice—only surrender, fierce and tender all at once. David looked at her and nodded, his throat too tight for words. In her weakness, she had found a strength greater than his own, and he knew then that this fragile bargain—loss and gift bound together—would define the rest of their days.

Chapter Thirty-Five
Threading

"Mama!" Eli's voice rang out, full of pride as he took his first unsteady steps across the living room.

Ana clapped her hands, her eyes shining. "Bravo, dyto, my baby! You're growing so fast."

David smiled from the doorway, watching his son with quiet joy. "Soon he'll be running circles around us both."

Next fall, Eli chased a flock of pigeons in Central Park, laughter bubbling from his small chest.

"Catch me if you can!" he shouted, darting through the fallen leaves.

Ana called after him, "Be careful, Eli! Don't go too far."

David ruffled Eli's hair as he returned, breathless and grinning. "That's my boy, my motek. Always fearless."

They often used Hebrew, Yiddish, or Ukrainian at home—sometimes even Italian—but never German. That silence was its own kind of remembering.

One afternoon, as they walked home from the park, Ana noticed David pause at the corner, his hand briefly pressed to his chest.

"You okay?" she asked, her voice light but alert.

"Just a stitch," he said with a smile that didn't quite reach his eyes. "Getting old, maybe."

But later that evening, as he read to Eli from a colourful picture book, Ana watched his breathing—just a little shallower than usual, his voice a little slower.

One evening, after a long day, Eli curled up on Ana's lap. She stroked his hair softly and hummed a lullaby in Yiddish.

David slumped in his favourite armchair, glanced over, and whispered, "She sings it just like our mothers did."

Eli's eyes fluttered closed, the world melting into the rhythm of his mother's voice.

At the dinner table, the clatter of dishes mixed with chatter.

"Tell me again, Papa," Eli begged, "How did you and Mama meet?"

David chuckled, glancing at Ana. "Well, it's a long story, but it starts with a scarf…"

Ana smiled, reaching out to squeeze David's hand. "A scarf that carried all our hopes."

Later, Eli's scribbles covered the kitchen table.

"Is that a Soviet rocket?" Ana asked, examining the colourful chaos.

Eli nodded seriously. "Going to the stars someday."

On a Saturday morning, just before going to synagogue, David showed Eli how to tie a tie.

"Like this, Eli," he said patiently.

Eli frowned, concentrating. "It's tricky."

"Just like life," David smiled, "but worth the effort."

Later that night, Eli whispered, "I love you, Mama."

Ana kissed his forehead, her voice hushed with awe. "I love you more than all the stars combined. Tykho, moye dytyo." She touched his cheek, barely a breath: "Baruch Hashem. He's safe."

This is life, she thought. Fragile and fierce, beautiful beyond words.

In a family photo, placed gently on Eli's dresser, their faces glowed—hope, love, and the quiet strength of survival captured forever, threaded together by what endured.

Chapter Thirty-Six
Past

"Mama! Look what I found!" Eli's voice rang out as he darted into the kitchen, clutching something tightly in his hand.

Ana turned from the stove, already sensing the pull of something old. "What is it, dyto?"

He set it carefully on the table. A small cloth pouch—faded, hand—stitched, the seams frayed and smooth with age. She recognized it immediately.

She walked over slowly, heart catching. "Where did you find this?"

"In the sewing tin. The bottom part. I think it was tucked under the lining."

Ana stared at it for a moment, then reached for the drawstring. Her fingers hesitated, then gently pulled it open.

Inside: the photograph. Three girls. Their hair was neatly parted, and ribbons were tied. They stood shoulder to shoulder in front of a modest shop with a striped awning, sunlight caught in the glass behind them. The eldest stood with one hand protectively behind the others, her gaze steady and fierce. All three wore their best dresses, their shoes polished, and their posture proud. Their innocence was unbroken, as though the shutter had sealed them in safety.

David entered from the hallway, "What's going on?"

Ana didn't look up. She held the photograph in both hands, then lifted it toward him.

He took it—absently at first—and then froze. The colour drained from his face.

His voice, when it came, was almost inaudible. "How did you get this?"

"It was Malka's," Ana said quietly. "She kept it with her, always. Hidden in her mattress, at the camp."

David stared at the image, his hand beginning to tremble. "I know them. I-" his voice caught. "They were my girls."

He touched each face with a fingertip, one by one, as if counting the years backward. "Rivka. Tova. Miriam."

Ana stood silent beside him. The room felt suspended, like breath before a sob.

"I never saw them," she said gently. "They were already gone when I met her."

David sat down slowly, still holding the photo. "I didn't know. After the war was over—I came back. I tried everything-Red Cross, tracing names, lists, survivors. Went to… Went back… Home… I found nothing. Just that they'd been taken." He swallowed. "I kept hoping…"

"She didn't speak of them often," Ana said. "But she showed me this photo once. When I needed a reminder that life before was not gone, it was just not here anymore. A moment of remembering. She called it a way to stay human."

David gave a slight nod, his throat working. "Rivka was always singing. She made up songs on the walk to school. Tova… she wanted to be a teacher. She made lesson plans for her sisters, even if they didn't want to learn. And Miriam…" He paused. "She was the youngest. She followed the others like a shadow. Always clutching a doll with the blue wide open eyes."

He was silent for a long while.

"She saved me, David. She held me when I thought I could not go on. I owe her more than I can ever repay." Ana said it and touched David's hand.

Eli leaned against Ana, eyes wide, uncertain.

Then, softly, Ana spoke about this revelation that ripped the old scars open. "Malka was your wife."

David looked up. "Yes."

Her hand is still touching his. Then he slowly squeezed her hand. Tight, then tighter.

"And now," Ana said, as a matter of fact, "you're here. With me. With us."

He nodded slowly. "I've thought about it more times than I can say. Whether it was strange. Whether it dishonours what we had." He looked down again at the photograph. "But the truth is… it doesn't. There is no replacing. No redoing. There is only living. Carrying forward what still breathes."

Ana's eyes shimmered, but she said nothing.

David went on, quietly. "Malka was love. And loss. You are… something that still dares to be. Love and loved. Living."

Ana reached for the pouch, folded it with care, and placed it in David's open palm. He held it gently, like a prayer.

"She kept them with her," Ana said. "All the way through."

"She did," he whispered. "You did. And now we do."

Eli stood still as he knew not to ask questions about the past. They would not be answered and passed over as if the parents believed that some scars should remain covered.

Outside, the wind moved through the trees—a hush, a hush, a hush. Inside, the past did not vanish or fade. It settled into its rightful place.

Not erased, not undone, not found, but unearthed. The new growth did not tremble at what lay beneath; instead, it felt the roots entwine in gratitude—accepting, carrying forward, and blessing the life still being lived.

Chapter Thirty-Seven
Present

The years slipped by not in silence, but in the music of an ordinary life finally allowed to bloom.

Eli's laughter filled the apartment, bouncing off the walls as he grew taller, his steps heavier. Once, Ana and David returned early from the factory to find him sprawled on the couch with a flashlight, deep in a book he wasn't supposed to read after bedtime. He startled upright, cheeks red, stammering excuses, and David only chuckled, ruffling his son's hair.

Ana shook her head and smiled, "This is what we prayed for," she thought.

At the factory, Ana's role deepened. What had begun as careful oversight became authority. She bought a small warehouse on the Lower East Side, then another uptown. She learned the rhythm of the real estate market the way she had once learned stitches—patient, precise, deliberate.

She still cooked, cleaned her apartment, and bought all her groceries, which were now delivered. Mrs. Chan, who had just opened a shop on the corner of her street, did her laundry. Ana didn't mind the house and factory work, as it filled her days with movement and quiet happiness.

On Saturdays, she worked at the synagogue, helping in the kitchen, folding prayer shawls, and making sure no one left hungry. She carried herself with quiet dignity, never asking for praise, content with the simple weight of being useful.

One evening, Ana and David found themselves laughing in the quiet of their bedroom, their laughter tumbling into something softer. After so many years of holding each other through grief, they still reached for each other with a hunger that was not desperation but devotion. David kissed the hollow of her collarbone, whispering something in Yiddish that made her smile in the half—dark. She gently lowered herself onto him, their bodies moving in quiet rhythm—hands gliding, lips brushing, laughter dissolving into breath.

The door creaked.

"Mama?" Eli's small voice called before his eyes adjusted to the room.

Ana startled, rolled off and pulled the sheet up quickly. David lay beside her, both stifling laughter and embarrassment. Eli froze in the doorway, wide—eyed.

"I—I just wanted a glass of water," he stammered.

David sat up, his voice calm but amused. "And you shall have it, motek. But next time, you knock first, hm?"

Ana, cheeks flushed but eyes kind, reached out a hand. "Go on, dytyo. The kitchen is yours."

Eli hesitated, then scurried away, the sound of his bare feet pattering down the hall.

When the door clicked shut again, Ana leaned against David's chest, both of them shaking with laughter.

"He will never forgive us," she whispered.

"He will," David murmured, kissing the top of her head. "One day, he will understand. When he meets the right girl."

In the morning, nobody talked about the previous night. David quietly pulled the human body encyclopedia from the shelf and set it before Eli.

Eli gazed at him and whispered, "Okay, I think I am okay." He took the book and put it in his backpack.

Ana brushed his hair and kissed him. She was not a hugger.

But David seemed to exhale into this new life as if it were something he had done before, and the memory of it returned. He no longer carried the restlessness of a man searching for what he had lost. Instead, he held a contentment that surprised even him. He walked Eli to school in the mornings, waiting on the sidewalk until his son disappeared inside. He read newspapers slowly in the evenings, sometimes aloud, sometimes just humming. He no longer lived in survival. He lived in the presence.

Eli was shy, yes, but his mind was sharp. He studied hard, often falling asleep at his desk with a pencil still in hand. At synagogue, he listened more than he spoke, eyes wide, absorbing. The rabbi called him "a boy of questions"-the kind that stretch beyond the page. At home, he trailed Ana through the rooms, watching how she folded linens, measured fabric, and balanced the books with neat columns. He spent his breaks at the factory, observing, learning the trade, and keeping the ledgers.

"You'll need to know this one day," she told him, and he nodded solemnly, as though the world already waited for him.

One spring afternoon, the three of them walked through Central Park. Cherry blossoms had dusted the air pink and white, and Eli darted ahead, chasing pigeons like he once had as a toddler. When he turned back, grinning, Ana and David walked hand in hand, slower now, but steady. For a moment, Eli stopped and just watched them, something soft dawning in his young face. Then he ran back, slipping his small hand into theirs, binding the three of them together.

That night, after Eli had gone to bed, Ana stood by the window, looking out over the city lights. David came up behind her, wrapping his arms around her waist, resting his chin on her shoulder.

"Do you realize?" he murmured.

"What?"

"We have everything."

Ana closed her eyes, letting the truth of it sink in. For once, there was no storm at the door, no dread waiting at the threshold—just a family, whole and living. And for the first time in her life, Ana started to believe in the word "present".

Chapter Thirty-Eight
A Rite of Passage

The synagogue was bathed in golden light, the late afternoon sun slanting through the stained glass and painting the pews in colour. Eli stood at the bimah, his tallit newly draped around his thin shoulders, slightly too long, the fringe brushing his wrists. His fingers gripped the edge of the reading stand, knuckles pale.

"Today," the rabbi said gently, his voice warm but firm, "you become a man in the eyes of our people."

Eli nodded, wide—eyed but steady. He took a breath that was almost a prayer and began to chant. His voice, unsure at first, gathered strength as the ancient melody carried him.

Ana sat still, almost as if scared to breathe, hands clasped an unopened prayer book in her lap. She watched Eli's lips move, the familiar cadence rising through the vaulted sanctuary like breath returning to a body. Her eyes filled with quiet tears. Her hair, streaked with silver, was pinned in a careful bun.

David sat motionless beside her, his face serene, a small smile at the corner of his mouth. He held her hand in his, his grip warm but looser than usual.

The aliyah concluded. The congregation murmured yasher koach and nodded their approval. A young man now.

The reception was held in a lavishly decorated hall just a few blocks away. The long tables were covered in white linen and blue ribbons. A tray of sugared cannoli sat where almonds usually would-Ana's quiet revision of tradition and a secret nod to their meeting place.

There was music, of course—a klezmer trio in the corner, and later, some jazz that Eli liked. Children danced. Women carried platters back and forth. Laughter swelled to the ceiling like lifted prayers.

Ana watched it all with quiet, glowing joy. She gave a short toast—short because she couldn't have spoken longer. Her voice trembled, her accent thickening with feeling, and the English words suddenly became unfamiliar on her tongue.

"To Eli," she said, raising her glass. "May you carry light in your hands, even when the world forgets where it is."

David added, lifting his own: "May you never forget who you are, and never forget where you come from—but always step forward."

Glasses clinked. People clapped. For a moment, joy held the room.

Later, at home, shoes were kicked off, jackets shed. The warmth of the day lingered in their small sanctuary. Eli was in his bedroom, humming softly as he got ready for bed. Ana and David sat side by side—she on the couch, he in his armchair, the lamp casting a soft circle of light between them. The silence was companionable, worn—in like their slippers.

Ana leaned her head on David's shoulder. "You tired?"

"A little," he said. "But happy."

She smiled. "He did beautifully."

David nodded. Then he pressed his hand to his chest.

Ana felt it before she saw it—the way his breath hitched, not with emotion but something else. A pause. A falter.

"David?" she said.

His hand tightened. He leaned forward, lips parted. Then winced.

"David-"

He gasped and sank back, eyes fluttering, the colour draining from his face.

"Eli!" Ana called out, already on her knees beside him. "Call an ambulance!"

Eli ran in. One look and he froze.

"Now!" she shouted.

He turned, fumbled with the phone, his hands shaking.

Ana held David's face in her hands, her voice breaking into pieces, tears blurring her vision as the world spun out of control. "Stay with me. Stay with us. Please."

The house, their sanctuary, their quiet place of rebuilding—cracked wide open.

And still, even in the rupture, they were a family, happy in the fleeting moment, unaware of what was to come.

Chapter Thirty-Nine
Rupture

The sterile hum of fluorescent lights filled the hospital corridor. Ana sat unmoving in a hard, cold chair, her coat still on, hands clenched together as if in prayer—though no words came.

Eli sat beside her, silent, too still for a boy of thirteen. A nurse passed. Then a doctor. Then nothing. At last, a door opened with a soft click. A young physician stepped out, his eyes lowered.

"I'm sorry," he said.

Ana didn't cry. Not then. Her lips parted as if to speak, but her voice betrayed her. She simply nodded.

Eli's hand slid into hers. They didn't walk home. Not this time. A cab took them through the quiet city, past shuttered delis and glowing corner pharmacies, down long blocks blurred with grief.

The driver glanced at them through the rearview mirror. "Long night?" he asked, his voice gentle, as if he already knew.

Ana didn't respond. She stared out the window.

He heard her accent when she finally said, "Fifth and Seventy-Ninth, please."

"Where you from?" he asked, not unkindly.

She was quiet for a moment.

Then, without turning her head: "Nowhere anymore."

The rest of the ride passed in silence.

The apartment—once filled with David's footsteps, humming, and presence—was suddenly cavernous and wrong. The empty armchair by the window, overlooking the treetops of Central Park, was unbearable.

Shiva began the next morning. Visitors came—neighbours, old friends, people from the synagogue. They brought food and offered words. Many cried. Ana remained composed, moving like a shadow through the rooms. She poured tea, folded napkins, and nodded politely as people said his name in the past tense.

She kept the tears at bay, partly out of habit and partly out of fear that they would never stop once they started. But beneath the quiet was something raw, unspoken—a small flicker of betrayal. He left without saying goodbye. Now she was left to carry it all-Eli, the apartment, the factory. The long winter of it. Alone again.

Eli stood beside her, his shoulders squared. He poured tea, opened the door, and recited Kaddish with the men. He did not cry, but each night, his small body curled tighter beside hers on the couch.

On the last evening of Shiva, after everyone had gone, Ana sat at the window in David's armchair. The tea she held had gone cold long ago. Eli sat beside her on the floor, legs folded up under him.

The view outside shimmered with distant headlights and park shadows. Summer crickets pulsed faintly below, their song muffled by the glass.

"Your father…" she began, her voice breaking, "he loved you with a kind of love that made up for all the love he'd lost."

Eli didn't answer right away. Then he leaned into her, head against her shoulder.

"We'll be okay, Mama," he whispered. "I'll take care of us."

In the silence that followed, Ana wept—not just for David, but for every goodbye her life had asked of her. And for the first time, she let her son hold her.

Outside, Central Park breathed in its green hush. The city lights blinked like distant stars. Tired, enormous, alive.

Somewhere, another thread had been cut-David's. But hers remained—and Eli's. Still holding.

Sometimes, late at night, Ana would sit at the window with her tea, the lights of the city blinking below like forgotten signals. She thought of David, his hands always warm, his voice steady. She thought of Roza—not as she had known her, but as she had imagined her, year after year: first a child, then a young woman, then a mother. A phantom life, stitched over her own like shadowwork. And Eli. Her boy. Her thread of survival. Her second chance.

One morning, he found her asleep at her worktable, the embroidery needle still nestled in her hand, threads trailing from the scarf like veins. He didn't wake her. Just stood there, watching the gentle rise and fall of her breath. A single silver thread still shimmered where the light caught it—the edge of a rose petal unfinished.

The world outside moved fast—new buildings rose, people rushed, seasons spun—but in this apartment, life was stitched gently, with care, grief, hope, and love, and stood still and unfinished.

Chapter Forty
Whole

The apartment on Fifth Avenue adjusted slowly to its new geometry. One adult coat in the closet. One toothbrush in the cup. One pillow that still held the shape of two.

The bed felt too wide. At night, Ana curled toward the empty side, reaching without thinking. Sometimes, she would wake with her hand stretched out, still searching. It wasn't the warmth she missed most. It was the quiet communion—the way David had breathed beside her, steady and real, a kind of presence that required no words.

The silence now was deeper. It didn't soothe. It pressed.

In the mornings, Ana folded his sweaters and tucked them back into the drawer, even though no one had touched them. In the evenings, she set the table for three and quietly returned the third plate to the cupboard before Eli came in.

She didn't speak of longing. But it lived in the hush between rooms. It lived in the space where David used to stand behind her while she cooked, his arms lightly around her waist. It lived in the way her fingers brushed her collarbone at night, as if remembering the path of his hand.

He had known her body after war, after loss, after the places that had tried to erase her. And she had let him know it—shyly at first, then with something like grace. That was what death had taken too: not just the man, but the slow future of growing old together.

Still, she had Eli. She had the mornings he overslept and the lunches she packed with precise care. She had the teacher conferences and the violin lessons, and the way he still sometimes reached for her hand crossing the street.

He grew tall quickly. His voice deepened. He got into the best private school, full of pale boys with narrow faces and golden—buttoned blue blazers. Eli's Slavic cadence—picked up from her and never quite smoothed away—made him stand out. So did his silence, his sharp gaze, his refusal to be moulded. Ana watched him walk into those rooms with his shoulders squared, never quite at ease, but never pretending either.

She did not remarry. She did not want a man who wasn't David, or a man who expected her to be soft in the old way. She had been a girl and a woman. She had been a wife. Now she was a mother. That was enough.

And yet— some nights, she stood by the window with her tea cooling in her hands, watching the shadows of the park move below. And she let herself ache. Not with desperation. Not with bitterness. But with memory. With the quiet weight of having once been touched gently, known truly, loved without question.

She thought of Vasyl, of their little hut, their unbroken bodies intertwining every night, young, hungry and sweaty. Their bodies made Roza.

She sometimes thought of the ship, the way David had reached for her hand in that darkened hallway, the dance, how he had made her feel not alone, and how—impossibly—she had believed in their connection. Their broken bodies, weathered but still hungry for touch, melting their loneliness into a new life-Eli.

Now she was alone again, but not empty. She moved through the apartment with purpose. She paid bills, reordered thread, wrote letters to her supplier in Milan, and ensured the factory kept running.

She taught Eli to sew on a button, balance a chequebook, and say thank you without lowering his eyes. And sometimes, when she stood beside him as he slept, she felt something like fullness—not joy, exactly, but completeness.

A life that had been stitched back together, thread by thread. It was not seamless, not unscarred, but it was patched skilfully and respectfully as time passed, chores were done, and days were lived into something whole again.

Chapter Forty-One
Chance

Some people we meet by choice. Others, by chance. And some—some are placed in our path like a quiet answer to a question we hadn't known we were asking or will be asking.

Nobody knew exactly how Tosya appeared in America. By boat, by plane, or perhaps-Ana sometimes joked—she had simply walked across the ocean like Jesus. What mattered was that she had arrived, sometime in the hazy thaw between empires, when the iron curtain had begun to rust during Olympiada-80.

She had no papers worth mentioning, only a crumpled USSR passport from some forgotten corner of the Poltava region and a purse that looked like it had survived two wars and a revolution. If you asked her, she would mutter something vague about a cousin in Brighton Beach and then change the subject. Tosya rarely offered the truth outright—but she never lied, either. Just dodged, deflected, as if her past were a room too cluttered to let anyone in.

Ana met her by accident. It was around the one—year anniversary of David's passing. It was late—one of those muggy Manhattan nights when the city feels like it's breathing heavy, pressing sweat into your collarbones. She had stepped out for a walk to clear her head after a long day at the factory, still in her pantsuit, sensible heels, and a silk scarf knotted too tightly at the throat.

She turned a corner and heard it—soft, exasperated, unmistakably Slavic: "Oy, Bozhe… chto delat'?"

Ana froze; her heart skipped a bit. This sound of Russian—real Russian, not the learned kind but the kind soaked in bone—sliced through her like a memory. She turned slowly and saw the woman sitting on a bench at a bus stop, counting out change from a worn little purse, squinting at each coin like it might betray her.

She was plump, with the kind of body that seemed padded for protection, wrapped in too many layers even for summer. Her hair was enormous, teased and lacquered into a blond tornado that looked lifted straight off an ABBA album cover. She was a woman without a definite age—maybe twenty, maybe fifty. A body shaped by flour, cigarettes, and worry. And a face that had forgotten how to be soft. Brown piercing eyes. Smudged luminous purple lipstick. A bruise darkening one cheekbone and smeared mascara.

They locked eyes.

"Shto smotrish?" the girl snapped.

It was the voice of someone who had learned to growl before she could beg. Ana almost laughed. Almost walked away.

Ana had never been one for strays. Not the mewling kittens behind dumpsters, not the lost boys selling poetry in the subway. Pity wasn't a language she spoke fluently. Not because she did not trust people, but because trust needed to be earned, not given.

But that night, something in her shifted—maybe the ache in her legs, or in her broken heart or perhaps the sudden homesickness that the accent stirred—dawned on her, or maybe just a moment of weakness mistaken for grace.

She sat beside the girl and said, quietly, "U menya doma est soop i krovat." I have soup and a bed at home.

Tosya just looked at her and didn't smile.

She froze, dropped the change into her purse, smiled, and laughed: "A pochemu by net? Why not?"

She slowly lifted herself off the bench and then just followed Ana. Like a stray. Like someone who didn't expect kindness, but knew better than to question it.

At first, Eli didn't trust her. But teenage boys trust no one and question everything. They are fluent in excuses and complaints.

"She's too loud," he muttered after the second day. "And she talks like she's hiding something."

"She is hiding something," Ana said. "But that doesn't mean she's dangerous."

He wasn't convinced, "She called my violin 'lopatka.'"

"She said it looked like a shovel. That's not an insult, it's a metaphor," Ana smiled. "Sort of."

Tosya was housed in the smallest room in the house—hardly a room at all, just a boxed—in corner by the laundry with a curtain for a door. She was so grateful and didn't ask for anything. She scrubbed the stove, made borscht and perogies from scratch, reorganized every spice jar alphabetically in Cyrillic, and then declared the coffee "too weak, like soup from a sad babushka."

She had a voice like a train whistle and opinions she hurled like bricks.

"You call this cheese?"

"In Poltava, we feed this to dogs."

"How can a man have such thin legs?" (this last one, aimed at Eli, who blushed so hard he knocked over a glass of water)

Which led to her confused outburst: "Oy! Glaz! You break glaz!"

Eli blinked. "Glass, Tosya. Not glaz. Glaz is an eye."

She shrugged. "So? Still break."

He rolled his eyes. "I'm going to lose my mind."

Tosya patted his shoulder. "No loose. I find for you."

That was how they spoke—him in broken Russian, her in experimental English, both of them irritated and oddly charmed. They could spend ten minutes arguing over a word and another ten trying to translate a joke neither of them thought was funny.

Ana watched from the doorway, arms folded, trying not to smile.

"She'll settle in," she told Eli one night, when he complained that Tosya had ironed his shirt collars into strange geometric shapes.

"She already has," he said, defeated. "She tells me to clean my room and does the room checks. She even attempted to do your embroidery".

"What?!" Ana exclaimed. But strangely enough, she did not mind it.

"She used a stapler," Eli added flatly. "On fabric."

Ana covered her mouth, laughing. "Oh no. She does not speak fabric or threads, but she definitely can weave her will and charm into anything."

"Oh yes. Said it was 'modern style.' I think the tablecloth is traumatized."

Ana shook her head, still smiling. "She means well."

"She means everything," he muttered, but there was no malice in it now—just a weary surrender.

Tosya stepped into their lives like a tornado but stayed as a fixture—loud, loyal, and unmovable. She vacuumed at sunrise, cursed in three languages, and cried at soap operas she watched daily after cleaning the breakfast table and the whole house.

She never said thank you for being let in. And Ana never asked her to.

But something shifted in the house after Tosya came. The corners felt less empty. The air smelled like garlic and onions again, and something was always on the edge of burning. She sang to herself in the mornings—strange old songs from a village no one could pronounce—and yelled at the kettle when it boiled too fast, as if it had insulted her.

Ana began to wonder if maybe some people weren't invited in at all—perhaps they simply appeared, loud and bruised and impossible, and made themselves a place. Some didn't need permission. They arrived by chance, but remained by choice. They came smelling of cabbage, Belomor, and cheap perfume—and somehow became family.

And just like that, hearts once unknown and unrelated were stitched together by an invisible thread of belonging.

Ana looked at the mirror that had been veiled in black tulle last year. It no longer concealed grief. It reflected faces lit with life—her own, Eli's, Tosya's—and for the first time since David's death, the glass was free to mirror happiness. Again.

Chapter Forty-Two
After

The seasons turned. Time, like the scarves Ana continued to craft inside, unfurled in soft, intricate layers. Outside was different, busy, efficient, lean. She ran the factory. The men listened to her. The women trusted her. She learned the rhythms of shipments, the temperaments of suppliers, and how to spot a bad thread line from twenty paces. Her shoes were practical now.

Sometimes, after hours, she stood in the center of the empty workroom—bolts of silk stacked like sleeping soldiers—and let herself feel the impossible truth: this life was hers. David gone, the war over, her ghosts still restless… and yet she stood. She survived. She signed contracts and paychecks. She made calls. She invested, quietly, in a second apartment in Queens. A laundromat. Another factory. Once, she'd been afraid of the city. Now she owned it.

She fiercely saved and spent on the community that finally became her own, donated to the synagogue, hospital, and all good causes. But never in her name, always anonymously, as she didn't want people to know she was of certain means. And God knew of her good deeds anyway.

And still, on weekends, she embroidered.-soft silks, deep reds, tiny roses. Memory folded into every petal.

Eli was her pride, her purpose, and her quiet heartbreak. He was too much like her and too much like David, which made her ache. He was her boy, her thread of survival, her second chance, her tether to the future, and her plea to the past.

He had his father's posture, but Ana saw herself in his silences. The way he hesitated before speaking was as if he were weighing history and kindness at once. She worried, as all mothers do—but more than that, she watched. She marvelled. She felt blessed. She felt proud. In synagogue, she always watched the way the mothers looked at her son as if assessing him as a potential match for their daughters. And every time she felt he was on top of their list—polite, educated, soft spoken, obedient, wealthy and mama's little Jewish boy, not as an offence but rather a compliment to Ana to be raising a good Jewish boy.

He studied a lot, his books strewn across every surface like breadcrumbs back to her. She packed his lunch every morning—whether he wanted it or not. She watched him. And prayed. And bargained with heaven.

"Mrs. Marks, the guidance counselor, says my grades have potential. She wants me to apply early."

"You should," she said. "Your father would have been proud. But you should stay in the city," she said far too casually, as she refilled his soup. "Columbia is excellent. You'd be close. You could save on housing."

"I'd live at home?"

"We have hot water, don't we?" she said, teasing. "I'm just saying. I cook. I iron. I pray. What more do you need?"

Eli raised an eyebrow. "You don't. Tosya does."

Ana didn't flinch. "Yes, but I always watch."

He smiled despite himself. "That's comforting."

"I supervise. Like a general. With better seasoning."

"I don't know," he said. "It might be good for me to-"

"To what?" she said. "To wander? To forget how to eat? To date strange girls with no last names?"

"Ma."

He laughed. "A little space?"

"I'll stand very far away while I feed you," she said. "It's fine."

But that night, as Tosya cleared his bowl, Ana lingered in the doorway longer than usual. She had built this quiet world for him, held him through grief, and provided him with food and shelter. And still—still—he would leave.

Sometimes, late at night, she sat in the armchair by the window, cradling her tea, watching the lights of the city blink like forgotten signals. She thought of David—his steadiness, his hands, the way he used to hum when helping her fold laundry. She thought of Roza—not as she had known her, but as she might have become. A child, a woman, a mother. And always, she thought of Eli. Her son. Her thread of survival. Her reason. Her heart.

The city raced ahead—towers rising, people rushing, taxis barking—but here, inside their apartment, time moved slowly. Carefully. With grief. With memory. With devotion.

And then, it happened. The lions roared, and Eli saw his light in their light."In lumine Tuo videbimus lumen." Morningside Heights was far enough from Manhattan, but he stayed home as a good Jewish boy.

Chapter Forty-Three
Late

The campus pulsed with the low hum of late autumn 1985. Wind tugged at scarves and jackets, and students hurried between classes as gold and russet leaves chased them across the quad. Eli felt the chill only on the surface—inside, something warm had taken root.

He stayed late after a seminar on the totalitarian Soviet regime. He lingered in the hallway with a girl named Bella Caruso.

She was breathtaking—not in the polished way of magazine covers, but in the warm, earthy way of late—summer sun. Curves like ripe fruit. Eyes wide and dark. Thick hair tied back with a pencil. She laughed with her whole body. She didn't wear much makeup—didn't need it. She spoke English with a musical cadence, the ghost of Naples in every syllable. She was still unaware of her beauty and the power that it could cast over men.

Her clothes never quite matched. Her shoes were always scuffed. And when she talked about history, her whole face lit up like stained glass.

Eli was taken by her beauty and loudness. She came like a storm, and he stood still. He was taken under her loud spell, and she was taken by his quietness.

That day, he forgot to come home on time. Ana waited. He was quiet at first, then pacing, then baking. When he returned, he looked flushed, distracted, and unapologetic.

"Who is she?" Ana asked, feigning calm and stirring tea she wouldn't drink.

"Bella," he said. And smiled in a way that split Ana clean through.

He had never smiled like that before.

"Is she… serious?"

"I don't know," he said. "But she's… good. And she has the last name, it is Caruso," and he touched a tiny scrap of paper in his pocket, warm and full of promise. He called her the same evening.

Ana sat still after he left the room, the tea cooling in her hands. The silence pressed.

Tosya poked her head in, wiping flour from her apron. "Why such a long face? He is late, not dead."

Ana gave her a weary look. "He is not mine anymore."

Tosya snorted. "Pfft. Children are never ours. We only rent them. No refunds, no exchanges."

She plopped into a chair, crossing her arms. "Better you learn it now."

Ana almost laughed, almost cried. "But he smiled…"

"Good!" Tosya shrugged. "Smiling means he is alive. Let him love, Ana. Even storms bring flowers."

Ana turned back to her untouched tea. The words soothed nothing, but they stitched themselves quietly into her heart. She saw the phone cord snaking into her son's room, and then Eli's laughter filled the air.

"Let him love, and laugh!" Ana whispered.

"Amen!" Tosya exclaimed and smacked her hands in the air. A puff of flour rose, covering them both in a white veil.

Chapter Forty-Four
Electric

Eli had always been the quiet one—the observer, old soul. Even as a child, he preferred shadows to spotlights. A skinny, tall boy who read during recess, who memorized sonatas instead of pop songs and felt more at ease with books than with people. The kid who read National Geographic cover to cover, who cataloged birds by Latin name in the margins of his notebooks, who kept his socks organized by colour. A boy with neat handwriting, too many pencils, and too many thoughts. He wasn't shy, exactly—just cautious. The kind of caution that knows the world can surprise you, and not always in a good way.

And then came Bella. Bella Caruso. She crushed him. Literally.

She didn't knock—she barged. She wore her older brother's leather jacket over her Catholic school uniform and didn't bother fixing her hair for anyone. Bella, who climbed over fences instead of using gates, swore like a sailor in three languages, English, Italian, and Latin, and once punched a boy for kicking a stray dog.

They met by accident—of course they did. Eli was carrying a violin case and a plastic bag of plums, and she was carrying a stack of books. The rest was gravity.

He ended up on the floor, her books around him. She landed in his life.

"You always this graceful?" she asked, crouching beside him.

"You almost killed me," he said, brushing dust from his sweater.

"Yeah, but you saved the plums—both sets," she said, grinning as her eyes flicked from the bag to him.

He stared. And just like that, something ridiculous and wonderful began to grow.

Eli didn't know what hit him. He just stood there, trying to think of something clever and managing only: "Do you always talk this fast and inappropriately?"

She smirked. "Do you always think this slow?"

He smiled. She noticed.

"There it is," she said. "Your first joke. I'm proud of you, Quiet Boy."

They didn't plan to keep walking together. But somehow they ended up under the trees, leaves in their hair, the sky bruising above them. She talked with her hands, full of fire. He nodded too much and said too little. But she didn't seem to mind. She'd ask questions, wait a beat, then answer them herself.

She leaned forward to tie her boot. He watched the curve of her shoulder, the way her fingers moved. And then—without thinking—he said, "You have a very big mind."

Surprised, she looked up at him as if she expected him to comment on something else she had, and the other boys had always noticed first.

He did notice them, too. He saw everything about her: her chest, her smile, and her smell. She brushed his arm, laughing, and it felt like static. He had never been so aware of where his hands were or where to look. His whole body was tuning itself to her frequency—high, messy, electric.

When they parted, she handed him a folded scrap of paper—her number, a doodle of a bag of plums, and the name Bella Caruso.

Chapter Forty-Five
Different

Bella still lived in a tiny but loud house with her parents, four brothers, and a Nonna. She smelled like oregano, sugar, and hairspray and always had ink on her fingers.

Eli still lived with Ana and Tosya in a posh Manhattan apartment full of rules and books arranged by author, language, and tragedy level.

She called him "Quiet Boy" and "Professor."

He called her "Trouble, Zhar Ptiza." Firebird.

She thought his handwriting was suspiciously perfect. He thought her handwriting looked like it had been chased by bees.

Eli found himself waiting for her voice—scanning the hallway for the flick of her curls, the flannel shirt tied around her waist, the way she'd lean into a conversation like it was a secret being passed. She never waited for permission to speak, or to laugh, or to sit too close.

It wasn't that she made him brave. It was that she didn't seem to notice he wasn't.

She asked him questions that no one else asked—not about grades or plans or where he was from, but things like, "When did you stop being a kid?" or "Do you believe some people remember more than they should?"

He didn't always know how to answer. She never minded.

They found strange places to be alone: the music building's practice rooms, the stairs behind the student hall, and an old greenhouse where nobody went except them.

Sometimes she brought clementines and peeled them slowly, letting the smell bloom between them.

Once, he played a sonata that was gentle and fast for her on his violin, as if his soul and desire for her were singing the unspoken truth. She didn't say anything when he finished; she just leaned her head against his shoulder and sighed as if it lit something inside her on fire.

They didn't kiss right away. For weeks, it was glances held too long, fingers brushing by accident, her foot touching his under a table, and neither of them moving. But once it started, it came with a kind of wonder. Like they'd opened a door without knowing it was there.

In the stacks of the library, between Soviet history and art theory, she pulled him and kissed him. His back hit the shelf. A book fell. She laughed into his mouth.

Then she asked, "Was that your first kiss?"

Eli hesitated. "Not exactly."

She raised an eyebrow.

"It's the first one I'll remember."

Bella smiled, soft and slow. "You're strange," she said.

"You like strange," he answered.

"I like you," she said.

He tried to say something back, but his heart had leapt too high into his throat.

They were eighteen, but something about it felt older—like they were borrowing from a love story already written, but living it now with all the raw intensity of youth.

He noticed things he'd never noticed before: how her laugh changed when she was tired, how she wore rings only on odd—numbered fingers, how she'd bite her lip when concentrating and never realized she was doing it.

Sometimes, when she wasn't looking, he'd trace the curve of her hand with his eyes and wonder how anything could feel so new and familiar at once.

They didn't talk about forever. Not yet.

But sometimes she'd say things like, "If we had a dog, it would definitely have your hair," or "I'd let you name the kid, but only if it's something normal."

And he didn't correct her. He just listened.

She laughed when he blushed. He blushed all the time.

They fought all the time as teenagers do. She was all sharp corners and fast exits. He hated raised voices and didn't know how to chase. She hated that he never fought back and shrugged instead of yelling. He hated when she disappeared for hours without telling anyone.

But somehow, they always found their way back. With small things. A pressed rose in his violin case. A cannoli in a paper bag. A gentle touch of a cold palm under the desk.

He made her mixtapes of Russian classical music and Italian Opera arias. She cracked dumb jokes, and it all summoned a kind of quiet magic that neither of them could name.

She once told him, "You're the first person who ever made me want to be good."

He answered, "You're the first person who ever made me want to be me."

Once, she asked, "Do you think you'll marry a nice Jewish girl and forget me?"

"Do you think we'll last?"

He tilted his head and said, "Statistically speaking…"

She touched his lips with her tiny finger and smiled. "Then we just might."

And somehow, they worked. She made space for him. He gave her quiet that didn't feel like absence. And slowly—without trying, without planning—they began to fall. Not like a crash. More like leaves. Soft, steady, and impossible to ignore.

They were different. He was scared, but she was not. They weren't alike—not even close. But maybe that was the point. They were made from different cloths but perfectly paired together. Different, yes. Two halves of something that could be stitched together, seemingly to create something new.

Chapter Forty-Six
Dolce

Sunday was never quiet in the Caruso house. Loud and joyful, they lived up to the famous name. The table groaned under platters of roasted peppers, meatballs, fresh bread, and enough pasta to feed an army. Someone was always shouting over someone else—in love, in argument, in laughter—and someone was always telling Nonna she'd added too much garlic, while going back for seconds anyway.

From the moment Eli stepped inside, there was noise, heat, and oregano. A pot of something red simmered on the stove. Voices overlapped like music. Laughter ricocheted off the tile. Someone was shouting in the backyard, and someone else was singing in the hall.

"Put down the sauce, Gia, he's here!"

"He can wait, he's not melting!"

"Ma! That's rude!"

"I'm stirring with love, what more you want?"

Bella grinned as she shut the door behind him. "Welcome to the circus."

Eli smiled. "Do I need a ticket?"

"No," she said, grabbing his hand. "Just a good stomach and thick skin."

Gia—round, laughing, smelling of garlic and heaven—bustled in with a spoon in one hand and a towel in the other.

"You're the boy, eh?" she said, eyes twinkling. "The quiet one."

"I—yes," Eli managed.

"You're too skinny," she told him, pinching his cheek. "Sit. You like mozzarella? I made the good kind."

Eli sat. He smiled. He'd never known noise could feel so much like welcome.

"Bella says you read books and wash your own dishes. We like you already."

She kissed his cheek, then waved a spoon in the air. "Mangia, mangia! Sit!"

Dinner was an opera, a parade, a declaration of love made through carbs. Four brothers passed plates like arguments: meatballs, roasted peppers, crusty bread, caponata, and tiramisu in the fridge, "if you survive the pasta."

Bella leaned close. "Don't let Marco talk politics. Just nod and eat."

He nodded. He ate.

Her father, Rocco, a plumber with hands like spades and a voice like gravel, poured wine into everyone's glass.

"To Bella," he said. "Our only college kid. And to the boy-Eli. You got a good name. Simple. Honest."

"Like a wrench," someone teased.

"Like a prayer," Gia said, looking sternly at the joker.

Later, when the plates were cleared and someone had started an argument over whether you put pecorino or parmigiano on eggplant, Bella pulled him into the hallway.

"You okay?" she whispered, got on her tiptoes and kissed him on the forehead.

Eli smiled and nodded. "Better than okay. I didn't know dinner could sound like this."

"Too much?"

"No. Just… full." He smiled again. "In the best way."

They stood quietly. Her brothers shouted in the next room. Gia was already packing leftovers into foil, humming an old Italian lullaby under her breath.

Eli thought of Tosya's kitchen, which was filled with borsch and pirozki, beet—stained fingers, and flour—dusted aprons—chaos carefully managed under Ana's watchful eye.

And yet.

There was something in Gia's warm eyes, her soft "Tesoro," that reminded him—not of the noise, but of Italy. Of stories Ana had told in passing, about narrow streets and laundry lines, about meeting his dad. About kindness that smelled like oregano.

Bella nudged him. "You're thinking a lot."

"I do that," he said. "But yeah. I think… I think she'd like you."

"Your mom?"

He nodded. "Especially if you bring her a cannoli."

Chapter Forty-Seven
Hold

They came to the Fifth Avenue apartment on a quiet Sunday afternoon. The city below was a distant hum, muffled by thick glass and the soft glow of old carpets. The walls, still modest despite the address, were adorned with threadwork—always roses, each stitched in shades of memory.

Ana stood waiting in the doorway. Her hair with streaks of silver was pulled back in a low knot. Her hands were still, but her eyes, as always, saw everything.

Boots. Lipstick. Big eyes. Big hair. Big boobs. Young. Free. Whole.

"This is Bella," Eli said, awkwardly, like the name alone was a risk.

The girl smiled too easily. "Hi, Ana! Eli's told me so much about you."

Ana tilted her head, amused. "Did he?"

"Nice to meet you!"

"You too," Ana said, slowly.

Eli hovered like he wanted to disappear.

Bella grinned. "He told me you make the best tea in the city."

Ana nodded slowly, holding the door just wide enough, "Did he?"

She stood there waiting for Bella to take her boots off. Tosya rushed in and offered slippers. Bella nestled in them and smiled at Ana and Tosya.

They stepped into the room. Bella took up space—not loudly, but naturally, as if she was used to walking into strangers' homes and making them smaller.

Ana poured the tea with precision. There was no small talk, no warmth, and she passed the sugar bowl without looking up.

Bella tried. She complimented the china and asked about the lace tablecloth. Ana answered in clipped sentences. She asked about the factory and Italian merchants.

Eli fidgeted. He kept glancing between them, like a translator waiting for the fight to break out in two languages.

Tosya wandered in halfway through, wiping her hands on a dishtowel, and instantly sensed the tension. She gave Bella a grin.

"Pretty boots," she said, looking at the pair left by the door. "You stomp boys with those?"

Bella laughed. "Only if they deserve it."

"Molodets!" Tosya grinned. "Good girl."

Ana didn't flinch, but her spoon stirred a little harder.

When Bella left —polite, still smiling-Eli went with her to walk her home.

Ana didn't say a word. Just stood by the sink, arms folded.

"She's very…"

"Alive?" Tosya offered.

"…Unpolished," Ana said coolly. "And wearing that much eyeliner in daylight should be illegal."

"She's young."

"She's wild."

"She's in love with your son."

Ana stiffened. "He's eighteen."

Tosya shrugged. "And not dead."

Ana turned slowly. "Excuse me?"

Tosya walked over and planted herself by the counter. "Letting go is hard, yes. But don't act like you're burying him. He's not going off to war. He's falling in love with a girl who makes him smile like an idiot. That's not death. That's life."

Ana's mouth twisted. "She's not exactly subtle."

"Neither are you," Tosya said, hands on her hips. "You think your sharp tongue is invisible?"

Ana scoffed. "Please. I'm fluent in many languages. And sarcasm is one of them."

"Then use it on someone else," Tosya snapped. "You don't have to approve. But don't freeze him out. He already has just one parent. Don't let him lose you too."

Ana inhaled. Held it. Let it out slowly. Her fingers rested on the lip of the teacup.

"I just…" she started. "I wasn't ready."

"No one is," Tosya said. "But he was. You raised him for this. For the world. Let him walk into it. Even if the girl's boots are ugly."

Ana looked up. Met her eyes. Then—finally—laughed. Just once. Sharp. Bitter. But real.

"Fine," she said. "But I'm still hiding the good dishes."

"Good," Tosya grinned. "I'll hide the vodka."

And for the first time in years, Ana felt that letting go was not a crime, and maybe it would work out this time. Ana laughed again, sharper this time but less bitter. A fragile bridge was formed—one woven not just from thread or tradition, but from hope.

When Eli appeared later at night, he snuck through the hallway and into his room. He bumped into Tosya, who gave him a thumbs—up and hugged him.

"She already loves her, she just doesn't know it," Tosya whispered.

“Ana poured a cup of tea and didn’t stir the sugar in. She held the cube between her teeth and gently sipped the dark, hot liquid through it while looking at the city below.

‘David,’ she whispered, ‘how I wish you were here. I don’t know how to talk to him—about girls, about love, about sex…’ She sighed, the city lights flickering like answers she could not hear.

Chapter Forty-Eight
Bind

Ana stood in her kitchen, slicing apples for a pie Eli liked. She moved slowly and precisely—her hands were practiced and steady. The knife hit the board in a rhythm that calmed her thoughts, but didn't quiet them.

She heard Eli's laugh from the living room as he spoke on the phone. Probably Bella. His voice was lighter these days. There was a brightness in him she hadn't seen since David's passing.

She didn't dislike the girl. No-Bella was smart, kind, and careful with Eli's heart. But she wasn't Jewish. And that mattered. Even now. Maybe especially now. After all, Ana had survived, all that had been erased—her blood, her line, Roza had been taken and buried before the world had a chance to know her—didn't she have the right to want continuity? To want her son's children to carry not just his name, but his history?

Later that evening, as Tosya set the table for dinner, Ana finally spoke.

"She is a good girl," she said. "Sweet."

Eli looked up, catching the pause. "But?"

Ana sighed and folded the towel in thirds. "You know what your father and I believed. What we built."

"I know, Mama."

"And you know how much was lost."

"I do."

"She is not one of us."

Eli put the forks down slowly. "She's not not one of us, either."

"But that's not the same."

"I know," he said quietly.

They sat across from each other, the table between them. The scarf on the wall-Roza's Scarf—seemed to pulse in the warm light.

Ana's voice softened. "You are my only thread, Eli. The only living proof that I was here. That all of them were here. My mother. My father. Halyna. Roza. David. I want to see you marry under the chuppah. I want to hear the Sheva Brachot. I want to hold a child who will say the Shema at night."

Eli didn't look away. "What if Bella is willing to be part of all that?"

"Willing?" Ana said, a faint bitterness catching in her throat. "You don't become Jewish because you are willing. You carry it. You breathe it. You are marked with it."

He got up, stepped toward her and put a hand on her shoulder. "Maybe it's not about carrying it perfectly. Maybe it's about choosing to carry it at all."

Ana closed her eyes. She remembered the last moment she saw Roza. The grave with two names. And how, in the camp, what had kept her alive wasn't the past—but the belief in a future. That never happened. Now—her son. Her present. But he has his future. And now… his choice.

She opened her eyes. "I am not angry," she said. "But I am afraid."

"I know," Eli said. "Me too."

He got up and slowly disappeared down the hallway, the door clicking behind him.

Tosya entered quietly and started clearing the table.

"He's a good boy," Tosya said.

Ana didn't answer. She was staring at the scarf on the wall-Roza's scarf, still holding its shape. Still holding her, the memory of her.

"I used to believe," Ana said softly, "that if I stitched tight enough, I could hold the world together. A row of roses, a border, a seam. Something to hold the pieces."

Tosya didn't reply, only watched her gently.

"But fabric wears and rips," Ana added.

There was silence, but not empty silence —the kind of silence that lets you hear the deeper things—like the tick of the kitchen clock, click—click, like a train, like a heartbeat.

"He loves her," Tosya said at last. "You don't have to like it. But you might need to accept it. You don't own him. You made him but now it is time to let him grow. Not all fabric is stitched by the same two hands. Sometimes it takes a village to weave just one cloth."

Ana's hand went to her chest, as if something there had shifted.

She didn't answer. But she nodded—once—as if something old had exhaled in her bones.

She went to Eli's room and knocked on his door.

"Yes,"

"May I come in?"

"Not now, I am busy."

"Eli, just listen," Ana said, opening the door just a tiny gap to see her son's face.

He stared at her, "I said, I am busy."

"Eli, I don't like her—not yet. But you do. Maybe you even love her. Who am I to say no to you? Vasyl wasn't Jewish, and I still loved him. It didn't work out, but not for lack of trying. Maybe you can try. I'll learn how to accept her. Bella."

"Really, mama?"

"Really, Eli. Let her be your Zhar Ptitsa."

Eli ran to the door and hugged Ana as tightly as he could. She nestled her face against his chest and caught the scent of Bella on him— and, to her surprise, it didn't bother her. It felt as if she had already begun to grow used to it.

Tosya's voice cut in from the kitchen, half—teasing, half—true: "See? Fabric stretches. It doesn't always tear. Learn to bend, Ana—or you'll snap like an old thread. Better a noisy girl with boobs— no, boots, I mean, boots—than a silent house with ghosts."

Ana snorted into Eli's shirt. For once, she didn't argue.

Chapter Forty-Nine
First

The apartment was quiet. Ana had left early for work. Tosya was spending the day at her cousin's in Brighton Beach—something about a birthday and pickled herring. Eli had checked the clock at least three times before Bella buzzed the intercom.

When she stepped inside, the air shifted. She carried a tote bag, a bottle of cheap red wine, and a bag of canolis. Her coat smelled like the train and mint gum.

"Are they gone?" she whispered, glancing around.

"That… is correct," Eli said, shutting the door behind her.

He'd vacuumed twice. Lit a candle. Hid a photo of his bar mitzvah where he thought she wouldn't see it (she saw it). He wasn't exactly sure what was supposed to happen—only that something might. And he wanted to be ready.

Bella kicked off her boots and flopped onto the couch like she lived there. "So. We're alone."

"Yes," Eli said. Then immediately regretted how loud it came out. "I mean—yeah."

She raised an eyebrow, smiling. "You okay?"

"I vacuumed the ceiling," he said.

Bella snorted. "Oh, Professor. That's either adorable or alarming."

They sat close. Not touching. Yet.

The candle crackled softly. Somewhere downstairs, someone practiced saxophone—a tune was telling a story of love and desire.

Bella tilted her head toward him. "You sure?"

He nodded.

Then: "Are you?"

She didn't answer right away. She reached out, brushed a piece of lint from his sleeve, and let her hand linger.

"Yes," she said. Quietly. Then added, "But we can still chicken out and just make popcorn."

Eli laughed. "No popcorn."

He grabbed her hand and pulled her into the hallway toward his bedroom. She followed. He—unsure of what to do; she—unsure how much she wanted it. She leaned in. The kiss was slow. Familiar now, but still charged with that almost—electric hum—the way her breath caught, the way his hand shook just slightly as it touched her waist.

They moved with a kind of reverence—not for rules or rituals—but for each other. He fumbled with the clasp of her necklace, which had a tiny cross, and she swatted his hand, laughing softly. She unbuttoned his shirt with the focus of someone defusing a bomb.

At one point, he said, "Sorry, I-"

"Don't you dare apologize," she whispered.

It wasn't perfect. But it was theirs. Soft, fierce, young, willingly given, and respectfully taken. Both burning with desire, filled with the relentless tenderness of a love that felt like it could only happen once.

Her skin was warm beneath his trembling hands, a heat that sent his pulse racing faster than any sonata he had ever played. He tried to map her with his fingertips—shoulder, collarbone, the curve of her waist—but his hands shook as if afraid the moment might vanish if he pressed too firmly.

His whole body answered when her lips brushed his neck, arching toward her touch as if it had been waiting all along.

He let out a sound he hadn't meant to—half gasp, half laugh—and immediately flushed.

Bella only smiled against his skin.

"I love you," she whispered.

"I love you", Eli echoed back.

He kissed her as he had never kissed her before, and it pushed the wild rhythm inside him to a new volume. Her hair brushed his cheek, but he couldn't stop the fire rising between them. For a moment, he closed his eyes and let himself drown in the nearness of her—the salt of her skin, the heat of her breath, the pulse of her heart beating fast beneath his trembling hand.

Her body yielded to desire, finding his rhythm and answering it. She moved with him as if trying to match the height of his notes, a duet clumsy and fierce all at once.

What had begun as shy touches grew into something hungrier, as though each kiss and move unlocked a door neither of them had known was there. And in all of it—the trembling, the laughter, the fire—there was reverence, not for rules, perfection or performance, but for each other.

And afterward, she lay with her head on his chest, drawing lazy circles with her finger.

"You okay?" she asked.

"Better than okay. And you?" he whispered.

"Finally, not a virgin. Nuns would be furious and so would my parents."

He looked up at the ceiling, heart still galloping. "I think I have to marry you now."

She laughed—that rich, unfiltered laugh he loved. "I won't say no."

The saxophone player downstairs finally stopped.

They stayed like that—warm skin, tangled legs, a shared silent song that said more than any words.

Outside, the city moved. But in Eli's room, time folded gently in on itself.

And he thought: "So this is what it means to belong to someone."

And she thought: "So this is what it means to have someone."

They stayed in bed all afternoon, learning about each other's bodies and how to please each other. The sweat, the bliss, the heat carved their names in the book of love.

They lost track of time and almost got caught. Naïve, unaware of what the future would bring—but on this day, in this room, they belonged to each other as if forever. Their bodies, flushed and young, were stitched together for an afternoon—by tenderness, laughter, and desire—held in place by nothing more and nothing less than love.

Chapter Fifty
Happy

Eli's mind wasn't on schoolwork. It was on Bella. He liked how she listened. How she made silence feel safe. How she loved him. How she never tried to fix him or become whom his people wanted her to be. She whirled around him like a windstorm.

They weren't like the other couples in their circle—who held hands to be seen, who whispered loudly in crowded diners. Eli and Bella were quieter. More private.

She said once, "You make me feel like I'm not too much."

He answered, "You make me feel like I could be more."

Could he want more? Could he ask for more? Could his more become less for his mom? Could his happy erase her happy?

Outside, the city hummed with life—new beginnings, old stories, and the promise of what was yet to come.

Eli started humming. Not loudly, not on purpose. Just a low, tuneless murmur as he buttered toast in the quiet morning light, his hair still damp from the shower. The kitchen smelled like cinnamon and burned edges—the toaster had betrayed him again—but he didn't care.

Tosya, seated at the table in her flowery weathered housecoat, narrowed her eyes over her tea.

"You are smiling," she said, accusatory.

Eli shrugged, still humming, "Two hearts, Two hearts that beat as one. Our lives have just begun…"

"You are humming Endless Love. Oh, malysh, you are in love."

He turned, setting down the toast. "You know this song?"

"I am not a cavewoman, I am old but not dead," Tosya sniffed. "I have a radio. And feelings. And eyes."

She took a bite of toast and made a face. "This is a tragedy. What happened to your brain?"

"Nothing," Eli said. Then smiled too widely. "Everything."

Tosya waved a hand. "Ah. So. Bella."

He didn't answer, but the blush on his ears gave him away.

"You are glowing. Like an idiot who touched an electric wire. But… happier."

Eli poured tea into her cup and sat across from her. "It wasn't just… that. Last night. It was everything. It felt like—like we're in something real."

Tosya smirked. "In my day, we did not say 'real.' We said 'Do I want to punch this man when he chews?' If answer was no, you marry him."

He laughed.

She reached over and patted his cheek. "You are a soft boy. But good boy. Like sponge cake."

A moment passed in companionable quiet.

Then she said, more gently, "You told your mother yet?"

Eli's smile faded slightly. "Not everything."

Tosya gave a little "hm." Then sipped her tea.

"She will be fine," she added after a beat. "She is more flexible than she looks. Like dried fish. But she will soften up, with some tears of joy."

"That's… comforting," Eli said.

"It is true. Also, she is your mother. You are her son, even when you annoy her."

Eli nodded, looking down at his plate. "I just want her to be proud. And I want Bella to feel… welcome."

Tosya leaned back in her chair, folding her arms.

"Listen, moy zaychik. You are building something. With your own hands. Love, home, family—that is hard work. Your mother cannot climb into your heart and rearrange furniture. She can only knock on the door. Maybe criticize your wallpaper. But she will enter only if you let her in."

He was quiet for a moment. "You think so?"

Tosya stood, brushing crumbs from her housecoat. "I know so. I am old and always right."

She paused, halfway out of the room.

"Oh. And next time," she added, smirking, "change sheets before she comes back home. You reek of Catholic sin."

Eli groaned into his hands. "Tosya!"

She cackled all the way down the hallway.

Later that evening, Ana came home early from the factory. Eli met her at the door with tea already steeped and a plate of cannoli.

She raised an eyebrow. "Am I dying?"

"No," he said. "I just… wanted to talk."

She sat on the couch, took the tea, and waited.

Eli hesitated. "I know things have been… changing."

Ana said nothing.

"I love her," he said simply.

Still, no response.

"She's good, Mom. Kind. Brave. She makes me feel—like I belong. Like I'm allowed to be happy."

Ana looked down at the tea in her hands. "It's hard," she said finally. "To picture you growing toward someone I didn't plant."

Eli blinked.

She sighed. "I had plans, you know. Unspoken ones. A nice girl. Quiet, maybe. Jewish, maybe. Close. Understandable. I was married before your dad to a

Ukrainian boy, a long time ago… It was real, and this-" her voice softened, "—is real, too."

Eli swallowed.

"I see it," she said. "In your face. In how you hold yourself lately. Like someone took off a coat you didn't know you were wearing."

He didn't realize he'd been holding his breath until it came out in one long exhale. Ana's lips pressed into a thin line. She wanted to protest, to remind him of history, of promises, of blood. But when she looked at his face, she couldn't. Not this time.

Ana whispered, "Be happy, Eli. But don't forget where you come from."

"I won't," he said. "I want you both. In my life."

She nodded.

"And Tosya says you are a dried fish that would soften with some tears of joy."

Ana allowed herself the smallest smile. "Of course she did."

She reached for his hand.

"She can come to Shabbat dinner," Ana said. "If she wants. I'll meet her parents too, if you'd like. And if Tosya wants to bake the pie, fine—I'll let her do it, and she can even come along."

Ana hadn't seen the pattern yet, but for the first time, she was willing to add a new coloured thread to the cloth. Eli felt as if something steady clicked into place. They were stitching a new cloth—not perfect, not even, but theirs.

Chapter Fifty-One
Together

Bella's house was already alive before they even stepped in. The Carusos didn't just host dinners—they threw full—blown festivals in their dining room. The lights were too bright, someone was always shouting over someone else, and the smell of garlic, tomato, and wine wrapped itself around your clothes like a second skin.

Eli shifted nervously beside Ana on the stoop, his hands tucked in his coat pockets. Ana wore her nice gray wool skirt, which she had ironed twice. Tosya stood behind them, balancing a homemade pie and a happy expression.

"I told you," Tosya said as Eli knocked. "I bring pie. No one ever hates my pie. It brings joy and peace!"

The door burst open. Bella, flushed and bright—eyed, greeted them with the enthusiasm of someone who lived on a permanent sugar rush.

"Eli! Ana! And—oh, and Tosya?"

Tosya stepped forward and, without missing a beat, kissed both of Bella's cheeks. "Nice to see you again, the girl in boots! The little Italian hurricane."

Bella laughed. Inside, it was loud, warm, cluttered—utterly chaotic. Children ran between legs, someone was singing in the kitchen, and Bella's father was yelling to no one in particular about needing more chairs.

Ana froze for half a second at the threshold.

Tosya grabbed her hand and gently tugged her in. "Come. It's just noise. You've survived worse."

Bella's mother, a small woman with formidable arms, greeted Ana with a kiss and a scoop of salad: "You sit. You eat. You look thin."

Ana sat. Dinner was a blur of clattering cutlery and overlapping conversations. The table was set with heavy dishes: baked ziti, roasted peppers, eggplant rolled around ricotta, anchovies that Ana pretended to like, and far too much white bread.

Eli was glowing—not smiling—glowing. He passed Bella pieces of bread without asking, knew where she kept her napkin, and touched her wrist without thinking.

Tosya elbowed Ana and whispered, "You see? He's cooked. We've lost him."

Ana raised an eyebrow. "I didn't know we were trying to keep him."

Nonna, who'd had three glasses of wine and couldn't hear much, leaned toward Tosya: "You the mother?"

Tosya didn't blink. "Close enough."

More laughter.

Later, after the meal, Nonna raised her glass and said, "So, when is the wedding?"

There was a beat of silence—half joking, half waiting.

Eli glanced at Bella. Bella looked at Ana. Tosya raised her eyebrows like a conductor waiting for the downbeat.

Then Tosya stood up, glass in hand. "Only if I get to walk him down the aisle. He's practically mine now."

Then Nonna shouted something in Italian that meant Tosya's request was approved.

Ana—tired, full, heart unsteady—looked around at the table. She saw hands reaching, heads tilted in laughter, crumbs and stains and too much of everything.

Tosya raised her glass and shouted in her thick accent, "And now we can finally have the big Catholic wedding! And grandkids!"

Everyone laughed—even Ana, despite herself.

Bella leaned into Eli's shoulder, eyes glimmering. "I told you she was going to say it."

Eli just shook his head, smiling at the chaos around him. The Carusos were loud, joyful, full of overlapping voices and waving hands. It should have overwhelmed Ana—but strangely, it didn't. In their noise, she felt… safe. The kind of safe you don't recognize until your shoulders relax.

Later, after the table had been cleared and Bella's little cousin fell asleep in Tosya's lap, Ana watched the family move around each other like old dancers.

Eli walked past and gently touched her arm.

"They love her," Ana said quietly, without looking up.

"I know."

"And they love you."

"I know."

"You are stitched into them already. Quiet thread, coloured grey, into this wild fabric. But it feels right."

Eli smiled. "It holds."

Ana didn't answer, just gave a slight nod. And for the first time in a long while, the thread did not pull—it wove.

Chapter Fifty-Two
Schooling

The years blurred, stitched together by lectures, late—night phone calls, and trains caught at the last minute. They grew—not fast, not neatly, but like ivy wrapping itself around whatever was near.

Eli read in the library; Bella sprawled across his notes, doodling suns and violins. They fought about everything—curfews, grades, who finished the milk, and whether the Yankees were cursed. They made up in stairwells and borrowed beds.

Sometimes Bella stayed over, her boots by the door as a sign of her presence. Ana's neat row of shoes was hidden in the coat closet. Ana sighed but said nothing.

Tosya smirked, whispering, "Boots stay long enough, they belong."

There were holidays. Passover at Ana's table, Bella fumbling through Hebrew blessings. At Christmas at the Carusos', Ana endured carols with pursed lips until Tosya sang them louder and off—key.

Time passed in snapshots: Eli walking Bella through Central Park, her scarf tangled in the wind; Bella falling asleep on his chest on a couch in the factory office; Ana draping a blanket over them without a word.

Tosya told anyone who would listen, "The wedding is coming."

And then—one spring, the rhythm broke. Bella missed her period. Tests. Whispers. A doctor's waiting room. Eli white—faced, Bella staring straight ahead. Ana, beside them, purse clutched like a weapon. Tosya searched for a doctor who could be bribed to save the grandchild.

It ended early—a miscarriage, the doctor said. Or maybe it never took. The words blurred. Bella cried anyway, her laughter gone, her hands shaking as she smoked a cigarette she didn't even like.

Ana sat with her in the kitchen that night. No lectures. No judgment. Just tea, and a quiet hand covering Bella's.

Bella's voice cracked. "Now he doesn't have to make an honest woman out of me."

Ana's reply was raw, softer than she meant. "He doesn't need a reason to love you. Love doesn't need a reason. I know that"

Tosya barged in, poured some tea and shouted. "Idiots! Honest woman, dishonest woman—who cares? Nobody's honest after twenty. Life makes liars of us all."

Bella laughed through her tears. Eli, standing in the doorway, didn't know whether to laugh or leave. So he did both.

After that, life kept going: classes, exams, parties, and Shabbat dinners. They weren't the same, but they weren't broken either. The three years taught them more than books could: how to fight, how to forgive, and how to keep walking even when the path shook beneath their feet. They grew closer in some ways, further in others—stitched together but pulling at different seams.

Losing the unborn child taught Bella that life was short, and she wanted to experience it. So, after her second year, she applied and got an internship at the Museum of Contemporary Art in LA. She was there for two long summers while Eli worked at the factory. He visited her a few times, but flying made him very sick. It was the inner ear problem, one of the doctors said. Bella didn't come to see him because it was expensive, and she didn't want Eli to pay for it, so he flew to see her, to hold hands, and to be with her despite his sickness.

But as the years stretched, the seams began to strain. Eli watched Bella in crowded seminar rooms, her hand always raised, her voice filling the space with fire. Professors adored her, classmates hovered, and men lingered too long when she laughed. Eli felt pride at first—pride that she was his. But sometimes, pride turned bitter. Sometimes he caught the way her smile slid too easily toward another, and the way their eyes slid back. She told him it meant nothing. He believed her. Or wanted to.

Ana noticed too. Bella's edges had sharpened, not softened. She was no longer the girl fumbling blessings at Passover or blushing at compliments. She carried herself like someone rehearsing for a bigger stage. Ana could smell it on her—not perfume, not wine, but hunger. Not hunger for Eli, but for the world.

One evening, as Ana sipped tea and stirred the sugar, Tosya leaned against the doorframe, arms crossed.

"You see it too," Tosya said.

Ana didn't answer.

"She is already halfway gone," Tosya went on. "Girls like her… they want to taste everything. One man, one city, one life? It will not hold her."

Ana pressed her lips together. "Eli doesn't see it."

"Of course not. Love makes boys blind and stupid. He thinks she will keep him. But she won't. And one day, she will regret it."

Ana looked up sharply. "Regret what?"

"Not keeping him," Tosya said simply. "Soft boy, good boy. Heart like sponge cake. Hard to find."

"She aches for men—other men. To be touched, to be wanted. She craves it all, and not just from him," Ana said as a matter of fact.

"Who wouldn't want that?" Tosya said quietly, "Eh, who wouldn't? One strong man makes a woman happy. Many strong men? Very happy!"

"I forgot how it is," Ana whispered and sipped some tea.

"You did, I did, but these girls—they want to have it all, and the winner takes it all!" Tosya sang loudly.

"She will break his heart," Ana said.

"We will be here to catch him!" Tosya assured her.

Ana said nothing, but when Bella came in late one night smelling faintly of cigarettes and someone else's cologne, Ana knew. She didn't ask. She didn't need to. She just looked at Bella, and she took her boots off, and snuck into Eli's room without a word.

Ana walked to the kitchen and said, "Tosya, pour. It's already dying. Soon I'll have Eli back—but I don't want him back this way."

Tosya poured some vodka, and both drank as if they were grieving Bella.

Eli, though, never noticed. He only saw Bella's fire, her brilliance, and her chaos, which made him feel alive. He believed her love was enough. He didn't see that his love was no longer enough for her—and the cloth they had stitched together was already fraying.

Chapter Fifty-Three
Crossroads

The late afternoon light stretched long and golden over the park, catching in the thinning trees and casting soft shadows across the gravel path. The leaves had just begun to sprout—a slow, bright baby green untouched by ancient dust and the city's sins. Bella walked a step ahead of Eli, her boots crunching over rotten leaves, her scarf caught in the wind.

She stopped near the edge of the duck pond, watching ripples expand outward from nothing. A breeze lifted the ends of her hair. She didn't look at him when she said, "I got the offer."

Eli's chest tightened. He didn't ask what the offer was. He already knew.

Bella turned, face unreadable. "It's Los Angeles. The museum internship became a job. Real hours. Real money. They want me just after graduation."

He stared at the water. "That's far."

"I know." A pause. "I want to take it."

Eli nodded slowly, eyes on a duck paddling past them. "And?"

"And I want you to come with me."

He didn't answer right away. His throat felt tight. The wind picked up, and the light caught on the gold chain around Bella's neck—a tiny cross, a gift from her Nonna for her christening. She'd worn it every day since she was a baby.

"Bella," he said softly, "you know what's here for me. Ana. The community. The roots. This is home."

"I'm not asking you to leave them," she said. "I'm asking you to come build something with me. Us. A life that isn't just what you inherited."

"It's not that easy."

"I didn't say it was."

He looked at her then, really looked. She wasn't angry. Just… tired. Determined.

"I want both," he said. "You and them. The life we have and the one we came from. Here."

"I don't think we get to have both, Eli."

A silence settled. Not heavy, not cruel. Just the quiet knowledge that love didn't always mean moving in the same direction.

"I thought we were building something," he said finally.

Bella's voice was low. "We were. But maybe we're stitching two different things."

He almost laughed, bitterly. "So what, we unravel now?"

"No," she said gently. "Just… let the seam rest. Stop pulling at it before it tears."

The air around them felt too still. A child's voice rang out in the distance, calling after a kite. Somewhere behind them, someone played a saxophone—soft, sad, as if at a funeral. Not too long ago—though it felt like centuries—it had celebrated and blessed their union when they made love for the first time. Now, they announced the end of their togetherness. And maybe even the end of their love.

Eli turned toward her. "I love you."

"I know," Bella said.

"Do you love me?" Eli asked and grabbed her hand.

"I did. I think I still do. But I want to go. I want you to do it for me. You can come or you can stay. But I will go!" She pulled the hand away and stuffed it in her pocket.

"But I love you!" Eli exclaimed.

Bella didn't answer. They stood there, not holding hands, not moving—two people at a crossroads, the map unclear, the thread between them stretched but not yet broken.

Later, when Eli remembered this moment, he would think of the light—how golden it had been —and the warmth of the wind that attempted to dry his silent tears that he didn't even feel. And the strange, aching beauty of a stitch holding long enough to say goodbye. And the imminent feeling that someone had just died, but nobody knew, and nobody would be there to sit Shiva.

Bella got on her tiptoes and gently kissed Eli on the forehead. He pulled away. She shrugged her shoulders, turned, and walked away. Then she ran—her silhouette flickering between the bare trees until it vanished. Eli still stood there. Frozen in time. Alone.

Chapter Fifty-Four
Robot

The factory floor smelled like burned oil, cotton, and old metal. Even with the upgrades, it echoed with the same coughs of machinery Eli remembered from childhood—back when Ana still brought soup in a thermos and Tosya scolded men twice her size for spitting sunflower seeds near the belts.

Now, it was theirs—all of it—the factory, the block, half the district. Quiet purchases, slow work. Ana said it was about dignity—restoring places that held history.

"We don't buy to gloat," she reminded him. "We buy to keep us fed and warm."

Eli still clocked in. He wore a name patch like everyone else, drank from the communal coffee pot, shared cigarettes on the loading dock, even though he didn't smoke. No one called him "boss" to his face, and he never corrected them. It was better that way.

He moved like a machine. Wake. Work. Eat. Sleep. Repeat.

It was fall, but the kind that came early and mean. The wind knifed through his coat. The trees gave up early. The light was thin, reluctant. And Eli… Eli didn't feel much at all.

At home, Ana had taken to rearranging furniture and introducing him to women with suspiciously good posture.

"You remember Dalia's daughter?" she asked one night, setting down a plate of pickled carrots. "She's a dentist now. Smart. Nice girl. Laughs at all jokes."

"I don't tell jokes," Eli said flatly.

"She has good teeth," Tosya added, mostly to annoy him.

Ana continued. "Just dinner. No pressure. You need someone, Eli. You've been alone too long."

"I'm not alone," he said. "I'm just quiet."

But Ana wouldn't let it go. There were always names. Always stories. One girl played the violin. Another ran a community kitchen. Another was the granddaughter of someone from the synagogue whom she had once known in Odessa, which apparently made her eligible by divine right.

Tosya watched it all from the armchair, knitting like she was building a net for the sky.

One evening, after yet another polite rejection from Eli, Ana slammed a mixing bowl down so hard that flour rose like a ghost between them.

"You can't just rot here!" she shouted. "You had a future!"

"I had Bella!" Eli snapped. "I had something and I lost it and I'm tired of being stuffed into new costumes like I'm some kind of—of mannequin in your memory museum!"

The silence was sharp.

Tosya didn't look up from her knitting.

"Better to be a mannequin than a dead man walking," she muttered. "At least mannequins wear new things."

Eli stood, chest heaving. "I'm not dead. I'm just… I'm tired. Of pretending. Of trying. Of everything."

Ana's voice was quiet now. "Then go. See what's out there. If you're done pretending, go live for real."

He looked between them. Ana, heartbroken. Tosya, grumpy and wise, was already reaching for the sugar cubes.

So he packed a bag. Just a small one. A few shorts and shirts, some socks, underwear, and a pair of sneakers. A notebook. His passport. He didn't leave a letter.

The last thing he saw before the door clicked shut was Tosya's knitting—two colours twisted together, not quite matching but somehow holding.

And her voice, floating after him like incense: "Don't forget your heart. It's small, stupid, and breaks easily—but it's all you get."

Then the wind hit him like a dare.

And Eli walked into the world.

Chapter Fifty-Five
Rich

The factory had once pulsed like a living thing—steel, sweat, stitches. Now, it was silent. The last machines had been sold for parts, and the workers were given severance envelopes and quiet goodbyes. The threads were moving to China. Ana knew it before the papers or others who moved to the suburbs did.

She walked through the empty floor one last time, her heels echoing faintly across the concrete. Tosya trailed behind her in her enormous fur coat, one that looked like it belonged to a mobster's widow or a very pampered wolf.

"You know," Tosya said, pausing to pick up a stray spool of thread, "in my country we didn't close factories. We just renamed them after new dictators."

Ana didn't laugh, but the corner of her mouth twitched. She had become quieter in the past year, her elegance more pared—down. The suits were still tailored. The perfume was subtle. The pearls were still real. But there was something thinner in her face now. As if part of her—maybe the part that used to argue with Eli at the dinner table—had gone missing.

They no longer took cabs as Ana thought it was unsafe. They rode the subway now.

Tosya joked, "If we are to be saints now, we must ride among the people."

"Saints don't wear fur," Ana muttered, gripping the pole as the train lurched.

"Says who? The Russian Orthodox icons are drowning in velvet. Gold leaf! Jewels! Please."

They were a sight-Ana with her immaculate posture, Tosya with sunglasses indoors. Passengers stared, not always unkindly.

Ana didn't mind. In addition to the synagogue work, she also started volunteering at the Orthodox church in Brighton Beach, helping newcomers fill out forms, practice their English, and find jobs. They called her Baba Ana, though she insisted on "Ana" without the Baba. She lost that battle early.

Tosya came along, ostensibly to translate, but mostly to stir trouble and smuggle baked goods. They were an odd couple, the two of them-Ana with her understated grace, Tosya with her bluster and black—market wisdom. Don Quixote and Sancho Panza, if Sancho had a beehive hairdo and a cigarette case with hidden cash.

Sometimes, Ana caught herself glancing at the front door when she got home—listening for Eli's voice. But the rooms remained quiet. He had left in the fall, after a fight that cracked something open in both of them and split the seams of their family wide open. She had tried to set him up several times. Good girls. Nice families. He never wanted even one date. And then he just left—to date the cities and heal his broken heart.

"Maybe he needed to go find himself," Tosya said once, sipping her tea with too much sugar. "Men are like borscht—you can't rush them. Some must boil for years before they are good.."

Ana didn't cry. Not in front of anyone. But sometimes, in the quiet, she would open the drawer where she kept an old photo of him as a boy—gap—toothed, awkward, dressed in his suit with the tie that David just taught him how to do.

She was very rich now-Rolls-Royce rich—monetarily. She had bought the factories when the owners folded and flipped the land, but that kind of rich didn't matter the way it used to.

Now she found something else in the basement of a church, teaching a teenage girl from Kyiv how to say I'd like to open a bank account. Or teach little girls from Yugoslavia how to mend clothes, and in between, she healed their broken souls. Tosya would grumble but always show up, always bring pastries, always sit beside her like a tired, loyal knight in fur.

Maybe wealth had changed. Maybe it was never about the marble countertops or the clean balance sheets with many, many zeroes beside numbers. Maybe it was this: a subway ride—a day spent usefully. A laugh shared over a canoli. A friend by your side, ridiculous and true.

The cloth of her existence, once embroidered with life lived and life lost, was softer now, but no less beautiful. And on the canvas, the strange hands started weaving new threads—different colours, different textures—unexpected but strong and welcomed.

And hope—not loud, but quiet, the kind that keeps the door unlocked just in case—bloomed in both their hearts.

Chapter Fifty-Six
Healer

People say that time heals. They lie. Time does not heal; it is people who do. People can break, and people can heal.

Ana met Vera on a gray November morning, the kind that hovered in no season. The moment she stepped through the side door, Ana felt it—the hush under the noise, the ache beneath the waiting. She knew it too well.

Vera was sitting alone by the radiator, a thin girl with quiet bones, short curly hair, and a belly just beginning to round. She looked no more than sixteen, but there was an oldness in her eyes that had nothing to do with age. Her braids were too tight, her sleeves too long, her silence absolute. Her arms crossed slightly over her stomach, not in protection—but in denial.

Ana recognized that posture. The body was trying not to hide what it already held. She brought her tea, sat near her without asking, and said nothing.

After a while, Vera said, "I don't want it."

Ana didn't ask what. She didn't need to.

The girl was from a faraway African country, Rwanda, a place Ana had never heard of before, but would carry in her bones ever since. The village was gone now, or most of it. She had lost her family—mother, brother, auntie—some to machetes, others to smoke, all in the space of one burning week. Vera had been kept, not for rescue, but for use. Her voice never rose in the telling. She just named it as it was.

Then she was here. Alone. Brought to the synagogue by her Soviet friend, whom she met at the airport.

Vera was paper—thin. And carrying. While Ana had once been numbered, Vera had been scorched. Two different ovens. Same fire. Vera never said the word genocide. Ana didn't need her to. The silence carried it.

They began to see each other more often. Ana brought her warm socks and vitamin drops. She braided her hair once without speaking. Vera let her.

They didn't talk about faith. Or survival. They just sat, sometimes for hours.

She was placed with a nice Christian family who took good care of Vera, but she trusted only Ana. When Vera went into labour, it was Ana who stayed with her in the delivery room and then waited in the hospital hallway, pacing up and down for the new parents to arrive. The baby was placed via closed adoption with a kind family from upstate. Vera never looked at it, but she signed the forms herself.

"I want her to have more than the blood," Vera whispered.

Ana only nodded. She understood.

When the time came for Vera to leave for college— to some small town in Vermont where no one could pronounce her name-Ana went with her to the train station.

There was no bread and salt, no farewell song, no embroidered towel knotted at the edge—just the two of them on a rainy platform. Ana slipped a small silk pouch into Vera's hand. A rose was stitched into the fabric.

"For your pocket," she said.

Vera didn't cry. She just held it tight and said, "I'll write."

Ana stood back as the train doors closed, watching Vera's silhouette framed against the dull glass, one hand raised in a soft farewell. Her name-Verahimana, meaning "faith survives"-had never fit easily on Ana's tongue, so she had shortened it, gently, to Slavic Vera. Faith. In time, the name took root, and Ana whispered it like a prayer.

Another daughter, she thought. Not born of her body, but stitched into her life all the same. Roza, Rivka, Tova, Miriam. And now, Vera and her daughter. A family of daughters—lost, found, imagined, or gifted by chance—each one carried forward, each one sewn into the torn fabric of her heart.

The train pulled away, wheels hammering a rhythm Ana hadn't heard in decades. She stood there for a long time after, the rain soft on her face, her heart beating a little harder, a little older.

Every year, on the baby's birthday, a postcard came.

The first said, "I am okay."

The second was a photo of Vera in a pale blue gown, graduating from nursing school.

Then another: "Medical school. On a full ride! Can you believe it?"

Years later, a single line was written in black ink on a plain white card with a rose bush blooming somewhere warm: "I stitch hearts now."

Some people we meet by chance. Some we meet by choice. Some we carry forever. Some just come at the right moment to heal our hearts.

Chapter Fifty-Seven
Here We Go Again

Ana came home and smelled something… off. Not burned. Not spoiled. Just unfamiliar. That alone was enough to raise suspicion.

She stepped out of her boots with a practiced stomp and dropped her coat on the bench.

"Tosya?" she called, already on alert. "Why does it smell like men's cologne and… cabbage?"

Silence. Then: a slurp.

Ana turned the corner and stopped cold.

There he was.

A teen, barely a bird, still a nestling, —in a black turtleneck with cheekbones sharp enough to make a diamond nervous. Sitting awkwardly in her kitchen, perched on the edge of the chair like he didn't know if he was welcome or trespassing. His long legs were tucked too neatly. His eyes tracked the silverware like it might accuse him of theft.

"Dobryi vecher, good evening," he said carefully, as if testing the sound of the words in this rich Manhattan air.

Ana blinked. "Tosya," she said, voice flat. "Who. Is. This."

Tosya emerged from the pantry carrying a tin of sugar, as if it were completely normal to host unannounced Russian men for tea. "This," she said proudly, "is my cousin."

Ana narrowed her eyes. "Your cousin."

"Yes."

"What's his name?"

"Ruslan."

"Ruslan what?"

"Pushkin," Tosya said, waving a hand like it was a royal title. "His parents were poets."

Ana turned back to Ruslan, who offered the kind of smile you offer border guards—polite, wary, ready to run. "You're from where?"

"Grozny," he said quietly.

Ana blinked. "As in... Chechnya?"

He nodded once.

"And you just happened to be in Manhattan?"

Tosya snapped. "Enough! What is this, border patrol? He just got here! He needs rest. And borscht!"

"You brought a strange man into my home!"

"Your home? Your?" Tosya barked a laugh. "Who kept it alive when you forgot how? Who filled it with smells and sounds and warmth—not from radiators, but from life? I made this place a home."

Ana opened her mouth, but Tosya was on fire.

"You're cold," she said, jabbing a crooked finger. "You used to be warm. Like bread. Now? Chill. Like subway platform in February. No wonder Eli left—who could stand it? He went to find sun and love, because here-" she clutched her chest, " even the plants wilt from your frost!"

Then spat, "Suka."

"I am a heartless bitch now?" Ana hissed, trembling. "You bring some random Pushkin to drink tea in my kitchen, and I am the bitch?"

Tosya nodded solemnly. "Yes."

"I survived a war!"

"So did he!" Tosya shouted, pointing to Ruslan, who looked terrified by the entire scene.

"I lived through a camp."

"And he lived through Chechnya. Everyone has a sad story! You want a medal?"

"I want boundaries!"

"Then build a fence!" Tosya shouted.

Ana's hands clenched at her sides. She looked at Ruslan again. "What war?"

He met her eyes. "First one," he said simply. "I was thirteen."

She hesitated. "What happened?"

He shrugged like it meant nothing. "They put me in a detskii dom, the orphanage, after. In Perm."

His eyes dropped to the table. When Tosya reached to pour his tea and her fingers brushed his knuckles, he flinched—just slightly, just enough—and pulled his hand back like the touch hurt.

Ana noticed. Of course she did.

Tosya noticed too. Her voice dropped, sharp and low.

"The boys like him," she said, "the ones who walk different, talk soft, the ones who don't pretend hard enough—they don't just break their souls in places like that. They break their bodies too. And the ones who live? They carry that hurt like it's stitched under the skin."

Ana looked at Ruslan again. Really looked.

Not at the coat or the cheekbones or the neat hands.

At the way he folded himself small. At the image of the burnt past in his eyes.

Shame not for what he had done—but for what had been done to him.

She turned back to Tosya. "So what now? He sleeps in Eli's old room? Uses our towels? Eats our bread?"

"Don't be dramatic," Tosya sniffed. "He's not staying. He needs a day. A hot meal. Somewhere to breathe."

Ana stared and then said as a matter of fact: "Not again. Not another stray. Not another human with eyes full of war. I can't… I'm tired, Tosya. I want to be home and not to make memories, not to bond, not to have another boy, here."

For once, Tosya quieted. "He's not like David. Not Eli. He's not even me. He's just a stray."

"A stray?"

"Like a person no one claimed."

There was a long pause.

Ruslan stood, his hands trembling, then he pulled on his coat.

"I don't want any trouble," he whispered. "You have a good home. Keep it that way."

He nodded to them both and walked out into the Manhattan chill. The front door closed quietly behind him as he passed through it as a ghost, as if he had never existed.

Ana stood still.

It felt like a tear had opened in the fabric of the room—not loud, not visible, but sensed, like a thread tugged loose. Tosya settled into the chair with a long, theatrical sigh. Ana didn't respond. She just looked down at the empty cup.

Still warm.

Chapter Fifty-Eight
Afar

Eli left New York with one bag and the feeling of being unfinished. He thought he was running toward something, but it felt more like running away.

He first drifted through the Eastern bloc-Poland, Hungary, Slovakia, places where the paint still peeled from Soviet walls and the air smelled of coal and cigarettes. He taught English in cramped classrooms with broken chalkboards, history in Jewish schools where children's eyes widened at words like Auschwitz and Warsaw Ghetto.

Poland. Oświęcim. The iron letters arched above him: "Arbeit Macht Frei". "Work will set you free." He had seen it in every textbook, every documentary. But recognizing it in person, the chill of the gate under gray Polish light, made his chest seize.

He walked through slowly, boots crunching on gravel. Barracks leaned low against the cold. Barbed wire sagged, rusted, but still cruel. Inside, rooms were preserved like exhibits of grief: piles of shoes, children's dolls, women's hair cut into bundles. His throat closed. He thought of his mama, barely twenty years old, her braids too tight, her sleeves too long, the top with the yellow triangle and number sewn over where the heart was still beating.

In the archives, a young Polish woman in a gray wool sweater slid a folder across the table.

She spoke English carefully, as if each word might be misunderstood, "These are the originals. Please be very careful."

Eli's hands shook. "She is here?"

The woman nodded once. "Yes. Prisoner transport list, 1942. From Ukraine."

He opened the folder and there it was—the name and then the number. The digits he had seen on his mother's arm faded but were still visible. He read it—a line typed in bureaucratic ink, as if life could be reduced to digits. Next to it: "Holub, Ana. Age 20."

His vision blurred. "My mama," he whispered, tears streaming down his cheeks.

The archivist blinked, then, with professional distance, said, "Records show liberation in the winter of 1945. Fate unknown."

Eli didn't answer. He flipped through the folder and stared at the faded photo. A row of thinned, broken women in striped pyjamas, hair shorn unevenly, eyes too old for their faces. Among them was them stood a girl who wasn't yet his mother. A girl and an old woman in the same body, bones already hollowed by hunger and abuse, still alive. Eli's hand moved before he could stop it, reaching toward the photo. He wanted to reach through the decades, to pull her out of that frozen row of women and place her safely in his present.

Instead, he traced the silhouette with his shaking finger, as if to feel their connection, and whispered, "Mama, you made it."

"Please," the archivist said sternly, "Do not touch the document."

Eli pulled his hand close to his chest and whispered, "She is still alive. She is the girl on the left."

The woman's face softened, her professional mask faltering. "She lived?"

"Yes," Eli said. "She lived. She is alive. She gave me life."

Silence held them both for a moment—one guarding the past, the other carrying it forward—and now they were both tied by it together in the present. He sat there for a while, thinking of the girl in the photograph, what she had been and who she had become. His heart ached, but he was not ready to come home yet.

So he kept on moving. He read names on plaques, walked cemeteries with toppled stones, and touched walls where Hebrew letters had been carved before war and then silenced. He passed through trains, border checks, and hostels that smelled of cabbage and mildew. In Kraków, he taught children who clutched pencils like lifelines, wide—eyed at every word he said about history. In Bratislava, he boarded with a family who fed him potato salad and asked if America was as rich as the movies.

And sometimes, there were girls. Dark—haired, fair—haired, shy, bold—they kissed him in doorways, libraries, and platforms just before the train left. He kissed them back and forgot their names almost as soon as he learned them. They filled evenings and heated up the nights, but were never let into the sacred space Bella had carved inside him.

In Munich, he found the building. Not by chance, but by persistence—an address scrawled in his father's old address book Ana had kept, passed along almost unwillingly to him as a Rite of Passage.

The house where David Rosenfeld's first family had lived. Malka. Rivka. Tova. Miriam.

The shop that used to sell fabric was now a pharmacy. The glass was bright, and the white shelves were lined with aspirin and shampoo. It had the clean hospital smell of disinfectant and medicine. Eli stood across the street until the shopkeeper came out and asked if he was lost.

He wanted to say, "Yes, half a century lost but now found."

Instead, he shook his head and walked away. He imagined all of them—the sisters he never knew and his father, whom he remembered as a distant memory—and their happy lives—the Shabbat dinners filled with prayer, laughter, and food.

He thought Munich might anchor him, but it hollowed him out further. He wrote Bella a postcard from there, but never mailed it.

He kept on moving. Bosnia. Croatia. Serbia. Wars still smoked there—buildings had been bombed, men with hollow eyes were sitting on crates. Families had been torn apart, bodies had been used and thrown away. Eli walked through it all, helping and teaching where he could, drinking when he couldn't, carrying his sadness like an unlit candle.

Then Eli thought of going to Italy. He ended up in Florence, where David and Ana had once met in another lifetime, but it felt too golden for his grief. Yet he traced them there, hunting shadows of their beginning. He walked streets lined with laundry and sunlight, sat in churches where choirs rehearsed the same psalms as fifty years ago. He stood by the old tailor shop, now a bakery, and tried to imagine them, not as survivors, but as two broken people daring to fall in love after everything had been taken.

Then he understood why they loved it here. Italy was different. Italy was sunlight, even in winter. Italy was hope and a new beginning. So Eli tried very hard to stay and be happy in Italy. He took odd jobs: translating, tutoring, shelving books in a dusty Florentine library. He grew his hair long and tied it back. He learned to drink espresso without sugar. Still, Bella haunted him. He heard her in church bells, operatic sopranos rehearsing through open windows. He whispered her name in his sleep.

And then he met Francesca. She was tall, her posture straight as if sculpted by marble itself, her eyes the green of Tuscan hills, and her hair always pinned upward, a strand falling across her cheek no matter how often she pushed it back. She painted with fierce strokes, colours splattered on her arms, her blouse, and even her jawline. She wanted to live in fire, in appetite.

In bed, she was as relentless as she was on canvas. Their lovemaking was not tender but consuming—nights tangled in sweat and paint, mornings beginning with quarrels and ending with kisses. She teased him for his silences, pressed her lips to the invisible scars of his sadness, and demanded he learn how to dance in her tiny tiled kitchen while pasta boiled over. Sometimes he laughed, and sometimes he let her spin him, clumsy but willing.

And when she collapsed beside him, breathless, she would say, "You look serene when you pretend to forget her name."

But he never really forgot.

One night, as they sat on the balcony with cheap wine between them, she looked at him and said, "You like me, but you don't love me. Your heart is somewhere else. Go find it. Go find her. And when you do—don't let her go."

And he knew she was right.

Chapter Fifty-Nine
Mamma Mia

Ana insisted on taking the subway, even alone. Tosya called it stupidity. Ana called it Tuesday.

"You are not twenty, thirty, forty, or even fifty," Tosya said, wagging a wooden spoon at her. "You are not invincible. And you are not from Brooklyn."

So, one day, when Tosya was feeling under the weather and asked Ana to stay and not go alone, Ana laughed, "I survived a war. I survived worse."

And so she left. And out of all the days, nights, and years, it happened on that Tuesday on the way home.

The train groaned into the station like something wounded. Ana stepped inside, sensible heels echoing on the grimy floor. The car was mostly empty. Fluorescent lights flickered overhead, turning everything jaundice—yellow. At the far end sat a man in a parka, slouched with his chin on his chest. He was asleep, maybe drunk.

She hesitated. Then sat near the middle, clutching her bag in her lap. The doors hissed closed.

Another man was already there—thin, wiry, with pockmarked skin and a twitch in his shoulder. He sat on the diagonal bench, watching her. He smiled. Ana gave him a polite nod. The kind New Yorkers gave when they weren't quite sure if it was safer to look away or not.

The train jolted forward. She glanced again at the man in the parka across the car. Still asleep. The boots were too large. Face shadowed by the hood. A flicker of relief passed through her. As long as the threat was asleep, he wasn't a threat.

The smiling man moved—not suddenly, not casually. He got up and ambled toward her, swaying with the motion of the train.

Ana's throat tightened. She told herself not to panic.

He sat across from her. Then leaned in.

"Nice purse," he said.

Ana didn't respond.

His hand slipped into his coat. Steel gleamed, sudden and small. A knife. Not large—but long enough. Cold against her ribs.

"Hand it over."

Ana gasped.

"No—please! I have—nothing-" she stammered, her accent thickening under fear.

"No one's gonna help you, lady. Not even the Russian mafia's watching tonight."

She flinched.

And then a voice: "Hey."

The man in the parka had stood. Hood was still up. His voice was steady, marked faintly by a Slavic accent. Soft, deliberate.

"She said no."

The man with the knife looked him up and down, amused: "What are you—her boyfriend? Some kind of Brighton Beach hero?"

He took a step toward him, knife still out.

The other man didn't move. His hands stayed at his sides. But his eyes had gone very still. Not angry. Something colder. Something older.

"Let her be," he said quietly. "Is not worth it."

The attacker snorted. He looked at the blade. Then back at the man in the parka. Something flickered across his face—not fear, but memory.

He'd seen knives before. Too many. The blade didn't scare him. The boys at the detskiy dom hadn't used knives. They hadn't needed to. That had been fists. And belts. And worse. He had tried to fight back at thirteen, small, wiry, and too pretty. He had tried. But they were stronger. He had lost then. Not this time.

The man lunged. The knife came up. But the stranger moved faster—not cleanly, not like a hero, but like someone who had been hit enough to know how to fall. He twisted the man's arm, slammed him into the pole, and the knife skittered to the floor with a clatter.

The attacker scrambled upright, dazed, lip bleeding. For a second, he looked like he might try again. Then he bolted through the door just as the train squealed into the next station.

And then it was just the two of them again.

Ana sat frozen, breath ragged. Her saviour stood by the pole, breathing heavily, hood down now. His cheek was red and swelling fast.

Their eyes met. And in that quiet—she saw it.

"Ruslan?" she whispered, her hands still shaking, still clutching the purse.

He blinked and nodded.

The train pulled forward again. The silence between them wasn't awkward—it was something deeper. Something broken and newly stitched. They rode that way until Ana's stop. She rose slowly. At the door, she turned back to him, eyes glinting with something dry and knowing.

"Well," she said, brushing dust from her coat, "I suppose now that we're known associates of the Russian mafia, you should probably come along and drink some tea in my kitchen."

A smile pulled at the corner of her mouth. Not warm—but not unkind. An invitation wrapped in acceptance.

He hesitated—then followed. They walked in silence aboveground, through the night, past glowing bodegas and puddles of taxi light. For the first time in years, he didn't feel like he was sneaking through someone else's life.

He had saved her. And she had seen him. Not the shadow, not the ruin, but the boy still breathing under the wreckage. Whatever this was—however brief—it was theirs now. A small, sharp thread sewn through the skin of one night.

And he followed her home. She didn't remember how they got there, only the sound of his boots on pavement and the comforting silence between them.

When the elevator opened onto her floor, Tosya was already in the hallway, barefoot, arms crossed. She took in the scene: Ana's coat torn, hair wild, one button missing. Ruslan was looking like a ghost in someone else's clothes.

"Bozhe moi," she whispered. "What happened?"

Ana exhaled, brushing past both of them.

"Nothing," she said. "Just… subway."

Ruslan lingered in the doorway, unsure.

"Well," Ana said, turning back, smoothing her hair with dignity, "you saved my honor. I obviously can't marry you, but I can offer you to come in."

He stepped in and felt that he no longer needed to hide. They had seen his truth. He did not need to be accepted or acknowledged; he simply was the long-lost puzzle piece that fit seemingly in this place, not by choice but by chance, a second chance, to be exact.

Later, they sat across from each other in the kitchen. Tosya stirred sugar into tea. Her hands trembled slightly.

Ana looked at Ruslan—at the space he took up carefully, like he didn't want to make creases in the air.

"You're staying," she said. "Guest room's made up."

He hesitated.

She tilted her head.

"Well? You've fought enough bad guys today, Batman. Go rest."

In the morning, the apartment smelled like fried eggs and lemon floor cleaner. Ruslan came into the kitchen, fully dressed.

Ana was already in a suit, with shoes on and a scarf pinned. Reading the paper. She didn't look up.

"I need a driver," she said matter—of—factly. "And now when I have one. I just need a car. Can you drive?"

He shook his head.

She turned a page.

"Good, you will learn the right way. I'm too old for the subway and too Jewish to die from a heart attack in a cab when I hear the prices they charge."

Tosya crossed herself and spit three times behind her left shoulder.

Ruslan blinked.

Ana smiled and left.

Later that night, the three of them sat under the kitchen light, sharing a plate of Tosya's cabbage pirozhki and watching the skyline.

Ana said, almost to herself:

"A Jew, a Catholic, and a Muslim under one roof. As Russian an anecdote as it gets."

"Oy vey."

"Inshallah."

"Bozhe moi."

Tosya leaned back in her chair and sang loudly. "Mamma, mia, here we go again."

Chapter Sixty
Tear

It began with a sound. A thud, no scream. Just the dull percussion of a human body collapsing onto tile.

Ana found her in the kitchen, face down, her beloved green slippers knocked askew, one hand still clutching a dishtowel like it was a flag of surrender. The kettle was still hissing, but the tea was never poured.

The ambulance came fast, but not fast enough.

In the hospital, it was the smell that undid Ana. Bleach and boiled potatoes. It slammed into her chest like it had with David—the same beige walls, the too—bright lights, the endless waiting. A hospital smell that whispered: This is where we take your people and don't give them back.

Tosya did not wake up.

The stroke was "massive," they said, "catastrophic," a word Ana had only heard before being used in reference to train wrecks and war zones. And maybe it was that. A small war, in her kitchen, in her heart.

She sat by the bed while machines wheezed and clicked. Tosya looked insulted by it all—wires in her arms, lips cracked, her hair a bleached—blonde halo against the stiff pillow. It was as if even in unconsciousness, she was saying, Pff. What nonsense. You call this dying?

Ana whispered things she didn't believe. Come back. Don't be ridiculous. Who's going to judge my cooking and curse at the radio now?

But the machines did not answer. Neither did Tosya.

She died three days later, just after dawn. No music, no last words. Just the kind of quiet that leaves a permanent echo.

Ana didn't know what kind of funeral Tosya would have wanted.

When asked once, years ago, Tosya had simply said, "I'll be dead, do what you want. Maybe throw me in the sea. But not next to any Germans." Then she'd gone back to slicing apples for her famous pie.

So Ana chose the only thing she knew: Jewish. They sat Shiva.

The mirrors were covered, and a folding table was set with cannolis and expensive wine. Tosya would have rolled her eyes at this: "Why spend? People still get drunk on cheap stuff."

Someone brought homemade potato salad in a big Rubbermaid bowl. No one knew who.

There was barely enough laughter. There was just the buzzing noise of whispers, as if people were scared to wake up Pain. The house had so much pain; it was in Roza's scarves on the walls, in the good dishes and silver, in the armchair beside the window, and in Eli's room. Unspoken pain lived long and well.

Ruslan stayed with Ana all these days in his old guest room in the apartment. All the days of Shiva, he opened and closed the door for people, then sat beside Ana on the couch, silent, his hands hidden in his lap, eyes red, dressed in black. When people offered condolences, he nodded, murmured thanks, and kept looking at the spot where Tosya once held court—a flower cup filled with Russian hot tea in hand, housecoat cinched tight, a queen in exile ruling from the worn floral armchair.

"She used to make me put lemon in her vodka when she wanted to feel fancy," he said once, to no one in particular. "Called it her 'Kyiv Manhattan.'"

Her pale lips, her blue eyes, her white hair tied in a bun, and a slouch to her frame, as if pain had deflated her spine. She wore a black dress for the first time in years. Her colourful pantsuits, shirts, and scarves were hidden in her enormous closets as if they were witnesses to her happy life, and now, they were not allowed to be seen by Pain.

And then came in waves, the memories as if Tosya herself said, "Why this party so sad? Let's laugh, drink vodka and eat my pie!"

Then, the memories and stories flooded. Tosya was wearing a ski mask while cutting onions. She was pretending to be Ruslan's aunt, cousin, or sister, depending on who asked. Tosya was telling a very polite doctor to go to hell in three languages. She was blessing Ana's sewing with an onion and an ancient prayer that involved chicken feet. Tosya was laughing at Eli's graduation because she accidentally wore mismatched shoes.

"She said she was from everywhere," Ana whispered once during Shiva. "But she belonged here.

On the final day, just before sundown, the door opened. Ana didn't hear footsteps, just felt a change in the air—like a stitch being pulled gently through taut fabric.

She turned.

Eli stood in the doorway. Older, tired, and beautiful in that way people get when they've been far away from you too long. His hair was long and tied at the back. He wore clothes that she did not buy him. He smelled of sun and unknown spices, but his brown eyes were filled with apology.

He looked at the cannoli, the covered mirrors, and a young man he did not recognize dressed in all black. Then his eyes found Ana's. And without a word, he stepped inside.

Ana did not feel whole, but she felt as if Tosya had dropped the spool of thread from wherever she was now and said, “You can stitch it back.”

Chapter Sixty-One
Silence

The silence between them was not peaceful. It was not the kind you rest in. It was the kind that pressed against the chest, tight and awkward, like an ill—fitting coat you once loved but now could barely move in.

Shiva was over. The mirrors were uncovered, and the flowers wilted in their vases. The smell of Tosya's apple pie, borscht, and pirozhki was gone. The place smelled clean but sterile. Ruslan had arranged for the Spanish cleaning service to come every other day, but Ana never spoke to them as if she knew that Tosya would feel betrayed.

Even the Shabbat dinner was catered now. Ruslan and his boyfriend, who shared a tiny flat in Queen's, came to every single one.

Misha, a quiet boy from Moscow, raised by parents who were engineers and servants of numbers, graphs, rules, and science, had become an artist. He was soft-spoken, his cheeks round, his brown eyes kind and happy. He had escaped just before he was broken, and so his happiness slowly rubbed off on Ruslan and pushed the memories of detskiy dom out of his bones.

Misha brought potato salad, carefully packed in the large Rubbermaid bowl, every Friday. It was made with dill and love, Russian style, but it was all that Ana needed, wanted, and ate.

Life, as people liked to say with great confidence, was supposed to resume. But it didn't. It was as if someone had pressed pause on the tape.

Ana, dressed every morning in Tosya's housecoat, which was tailored to her figure now, moved around the apartment like she didn't know where anything belonged anymore.

Eli made espresso each morning and drank it without speaking, his eyes fixed on the window. They didn't argue. They didn't reminisce. They were careful, which was worse.

She watched him—her prodigal son, her ghost returned. He moved slower now. Wore linen. Tied his hair back. Spoke Italian in his sleep. He had lines around his mouth holding the stories he hadn't told her.

One Friday evening, after they lit the candles and ate, they went for a walk. While they were pressing their boots against the pavement, their coats closed tightly against the first hints of winter, Ana broke it.

"People started asking about you at the synagogue," she said. "Whispers. Like death had walked in instead of you."

Eli didn't look over. "And what did you say?"

"That my son had returned from the dead. And he drinks espresso now. And maybe he's a Buddhist."

He smiled, just barely. "I'm not."

Ana nodded. "You should've been. At least your hair changed religion."

They continued walking, now in silence. The distance between them narrowed, and it felt as if they were becoming a family again. The Manhattan lights behind them glittered like distant stars.

"I've been teaching," he said. "History."

"In Krakow?" she guessed.

He nodded his head. "Yes and no. But, actually, everywhere. Places no one can pronounce. Jewish schools mostly. Year after year. Moved when I couldn't sleep anymore."

"Being Jewish helped you not starve?" she asked, voice flat.

He laughed softly. "Yes. That, and I was good at making children care about dead people."

They walked past a man smoking. Ana didn't stop.

"You left," she said.

"I know."

She stopped walking. "You left."

He turned toward her. "And came back."

"Too late," she said and then paused.

"It's never too late," Eli said with a softness in his voice.

The words sat between them, uncertain which one to follow.

That night, back at the apartment, they sat in the kitchen. The kettle hissed, and neither of them moved to pour the tea.

Eli looked at the ceiling. "I kept thinking, if I stayed away long enough, I'd come back as someone better."

Ana looked at him hard. "Did it work?"

"I don't know," he said. "Do I seem better?"

"No," she said honestly. "You seem sadder."

He nodded. "That too."

"Was it worth it?"

"Yes, Germany, Poland, Italy, Slovenia, Slovakia, Yugoslavia…"

"Bozhe moi… all these places. And yet you are here. That is what matters."

He nodded and poured some tea for himself and Ana. They didn't hug. They didn't cry. They just sat there, breathing in the same silence, waiting to see if it would break and sipping black tea..

Inside the synagogue next Saturday morning service, a woman had leaned close and whispered: "So, is your Eli back for good?"

And Ana smiled, laughed and replied, "He is taken."

She hadn't explained—taken by the wind, by wandering, by something far bigger than a girl or a job or a lease. Taken by loss. And maybe, now, taken by return.

But somewhere inside her, Ana felt awoken—as the loss nourished by her silent tears allowed a new sprout of hope to break the soil.

And a thought crossed her mind: "It's never too late to start the new spool of thread."

Chapter Sixty-Two
Neon

The city smelled like fall or maybe spring (who actually cares when all the days are the same)-warm asphalt, rain, and old leaves. It clung to everything, even the sidewalks. Eli didn't mean to walk that way. But maybe he did. Maybe something old in him is still remembered.

He saw her before she saw him. She was standing outside the old café near the church steps. Her brown hair was streaming down her shoulder, still wild, but her coat was proper, dark and fitted, and her shoes—of course—Italian. It was her—her smile, her curves, and her loud laugh. He froze.

Bella. Caruso.

She looked up suddenly, as if an invisible thread had pulled her head like a marionette—and there he was.

Eli. Rosenfeld.

For a second, neither of them moved. Then she broke into a grin, which was exactly the same and completely different. It had more depth and mystery, as if it was filled with days lived well, with the voices of lovers who caressed her soft, sun—kissed skin, and the art she curated and managed.

"Eli," she said, like she'd just remembered a favourite word.

"Bella," he breathed, like he'd been holding it for years.

They didn't hug. They didn't touch. They just began walking, side by side, as if it had never stopped.

"I'm here for Nonna," she said after a block. "She passed."

She touched her gold cross, still on her neck, still protecting her.

"I'm sorry."

"Don't be. She was ancient. She'd say: 'God forgot about me on a good day.'"

Bella laughed and touched his fingers, slowly at first. He did not resist the forgotten touch. She slowly wove her fingers into his and pulled him toward her.

"Let's walk, eh?"

They wandered aimlessly, the way people do when the world shrinks to one other body beside them. The city had changed. But not enough.

A neon saxophone blinked over a closed jazz bar—soft blue and pink light glittered against the wet sidewalk.

"Do you hear it?" she asked suddenly, almost to herself.

"What?"

"The music," Bella said. "I swear, every time we're near each other… it plays."

Eli didn't answer. The ache in his chest was too loud.

They kept walking. They talked about nothing and everything. The years unravelled between them like thread from a spool—at first loose, then tighter, closer. She told him about cities she didn't love, the museum that she now ran, and the people she liked. But not about her lovers. They were erased as soon as their fingers touched again, as if an electric shock wiped her memory.

He told her even less. About teaching. About never staying long. About history classrooms in places no one could pronounce. But not about his lovers because it did not matter—she was his first and always remained his first, his ache, his forgotten touch, his Bella.

Then he suddenly stopped. Pulled his hand away as if the knot of time broke loose.

He looked straight at her, almost angry: "I loved you and you left,"

"I came back."

"Too late."

She whispered. "It's never too late."

He looked at her for a long time, then slowly reached for her fingers and grabbed them as if he did not want her ever to slip away from him.

"Do you want to see where I live now?" he asked.

She smiled. "Same place?"

He nodded.

The apartment door clicked open like it remembered them. The hallway lights flickered, dim and quiet. He led her inside, and she paused by the bookshelf, her fingers grazing the spines. Everything was the same—except the weight of it now, the shared history between the walls.

"I still think about our first time here," she said softly, turning toward him.

Eli felt it—the electricity—that unspoken desire, the kind that lives in the spine and the gut, that makes your body ache, that fills the air with fire and memory and want.

She was older now. So was he. But it didn't matter. The way she looked at him hadn't changed.

Outside, the city moved on. Inside, time paused. That night, nothing needed to be said. Nothing was rushed. The ache had grown tender over time, but it still burned.

The next morning, as Ana walked past the front hallway in her housecoat, her eyes dropped to the floor. She stopped as if she saw a ghost.

A pair of high—heeled Italian shoes. Red. Expensive. Beautiful. She stared.

"Bozhe moi," Ana whispered and smiled.

And for the first time in months, she felt as if someone pushed the play button, and the time started to roll again. She got dressed, put on her most colourful pantsuit and stepped into spring. It didn't feel like it was the fall anymore.

Chapter Sixty-Three
Oh, Boy!

For a while, it was like a teenage dream, sweaty, fast, impulsive, or as people say, hot. Eli and Bella were everywhere and nowhere at once. She has taken a sabbatical, and he was on summer holidays. Cafés, park benches, dim little theatres. Her laugh in his ear, her hand in his pocket. Sometimes she stayed the night. Sometimes she vanished for days. That was Bella—a gust of wind with Italian heels and a smile that would put any Hollywood actress out of business: innocent and provocative all at once.

Then, as the Labour Day rolled in, she was gone. No note. No call. Just the air after a candle's blown out.

Eli didn't ask questions. He'd learned. Love, when it's real, is often inconvenient. At least he had her for the summer.

Weeks passed—maybe more. The weather turned. He taught, walked, and thought. He kept the apartment quiet. The smell of her shampoo still lived in the pillows.

Then came the knock—just around Hanukkah. Ana thought it was the carolers from the building, who visited every year to sing the Joy of Christmas.

Eli was humming, "All I want for Christmas is…"

He opened the door, and there she was-Bella Caruso, hair a mess, oversized coat wrinkled, cheeks flushed from the cold.

Her eyes, always bold, darted away now. "Same place," she said.

Eli stared. His mouth opened, then closed.

Then: "You… Bella…"

She took her coat off and her rounded belly stared at Eli. He grabbed the coat slowly, hung it in the closet and looked at her, then at the belly, at her, at the belly.

Bella nodded as if she heard the unspoken question in his head. "The boy," she said quickly, "needs his father."

He looked at her belly. At her. His hand twitched as if it remembered her hand sliding into his. Then he laughed, loud and sudden.

"What's so funny?" she said, blushing.

"I'm going to be a father and I am finally going to make an honest woman out of you," he grinned.

She groaned. "Oh, don't say it like that."

Ana came to the door and stared at the belly, then back at Bella. Then again, at the belly, like it had a story to tell she hadn't heard yet.

"Do your parents know?" she asked, dryly.

Bella shook her head. "Not yet. I guess they won't ground me, but once they know, they'll never let me leave again."

Ana raised one pale eyebrow. "Mazal tov, teenager."

"I'm Thirty—three."

"You act like one. Came back, run away. Yo—yo at its best. And I stand by my statement."

Bella laughed, flushed and flustered. "I am sorry, I did not know what to do. I thought I was dying."

Ana just nodded, slow and amused: "Oh, it happened to me to. I thought I was dying when Eli came onboard. And I was almost a decade older."

"Do you want to touch it?" Bella asked.

"May I?" Ana whispered.

Bella grabbed Ana's freckled hand and pulled it toward her belly. She placed it gently, and then Ana felt the kick, then another, and then a faint heartbeat of the new life that was growing inside Bella's belly.

And it did dawn on Ana. The fact that she was not Jewish did not matter because the baby was theirs—hers, David's, all the people before and all the people after—a thread not broken, still weaving.

They drank tea, and Ana, as a mute witness to the start of this new union, listened to them talk about the baby, the baby room, and the wedding.

The ceremony was held at City Hall on a Friday morning. No chuppah. No grand Italian band. Just a foggy sky, two rings, and a judge who sneezed during the vows.

Eli, clean—shaven, no more ponytail, a gray kippa pinned to the top of his head, in a black suit, looking like a younger version of his father, David. Bella was not wearing white but instead a flowery dress and Italian—made heels. Her tiny golden cross was gently resting on her chest.

The Carusos came. All of them.

The four loud brothers and their wives, two crying aunts, accompanied by the three uncles, a cousin with a camera who kept blocking the aisle, and Rocco, who insisted on bringing a bottle of grappa "just in case the judge looked thirsty." Gia kept offering Ana cannoli and asking if she wanted to marry one of the uncles with a house, no mortgage, and a good pension.

"You will be set, dear,"

Ana laughed and kept quiet as her house had never had a mortgage, not to mention the blocks of real estate she owned all over the city.

The noise was enough to give Ana a headache. But she didn't mind the commotion, as if the past returned, and she was happy to welcome it back.

She watched Eli's hand rest gently on Bella's back as they signed the papers. Watched Bella blink away tears like she couldn't quite believe what was happening. She heard the laughter, the chatter, the clatter of heels on the hardwood. And somewhere beneath it all: peace.

She would be Baba. Gia would be Nonna. Very soon, probably before Passover.

And this thread—this wild, unruly, long—paused thread—had finally found its way home.

Later, when they returned to the apartment, Ana spotted them kissing in the doorway. He was smiling, she was barefoot, and a pair of Italian—made heels stood by the entry wall.

Ana looked at them, then up toward the ceiling, as if Tosya might still be listening.

"Bozhe moi," she whispered, a smile sneaking onto her face. "It's about time."

Chapter Sixty-Four
Arrived

The quiet of the hospital room was almost holy—not the heavy silence of grief, but the hush that follows a miracle—the kind of hush where even the beeping monitors seemed to step softly. It was dim and hushed, the kind of hush that comes not from fear but from awe. Outside, the city spun on—traffic, snow, impatience—but in here, everything slowed.

Bella exhaled. Long. Shaky. Her black curls clung damp to her forehead, her eyes glassy. "Is he okay?"

The nurse smiled. "More than okay."

She placed the newborn, tight as a loaf of bread, in his blanket, onto Bella's chest. His tiny face wrinkled. He made a sound like a protest, then calmed.

Eli stood off to the side, hands in his pockets like a boy at a bus stop. He looked at the baby, at Bella, then at his own feet, like he wasn't sure where he belonged. Then he stepped forward.

Bella looked up at him. "You should name him," she whispered.

He nodded. Swallowed. Paused. "We should name him Abraham."

The silence that followed was soft and full of weight. Bella closed her eyes. "I will call him Abi."

Then, from the hallway—

"Move! I hear crying! That's either my grandson or the espresso machine's broken! Mamma mia, we are late!"

A moment later, Gia Caruso swept in wearing a large fur coat that trailed just a bit too dramatically behind her, leaving a trace of perfume, snowflakes, and theatre.

Behind her, Ana entered in a designer pant suit. No coat. Just a scarf and the look of someone who'd already seen the end of the world and had no patience for dramatics.

"Where's my precious boy?" Gia said, throwing the flowers at Ruslan, who caught them with the reflex of a man used to chaos.

"Wait your turn," Ana said calmly.

"I carried Bella in my belly for nine months."

"I carried Eli for nine and then Thirty—two—and that in years!"

"I made osso buco through contractions!"

"I survived a war, buried my daughter and my husbands, run the factory, and raised my son."

Gia turned, eyes narrowed. "Let me hold him. I know how—he is my fourth grandchild!"

Bella groaned. "I just gave birth, but somehow you two are the ones exhausting me."

Gia made a noise of surrender. "Fine. But I'm buying him a Mustang when he's sixteen."

Ana didn't blink. "Baba already bought him half the city."

Ruslan stifled a laugh. He was still holding the flowers and a baby—sized turquoise—coloured paper bag with white letters.

Gia looked at Ana and then turned her attention to the baby. "What did you name him?"

Eli cleared his throat. "Abraham."

Gia paused. "And we will baptize him. In the big church. With the real choir."

"We'll see," Ana said smoothly.

"No, we won't." Gia smiled sweetly. "The choir is booked. For May."

Ana took one look at the choir—booking, fur—draped woman, and muttered under her breath, "Bozhe moi. Tosya has returned."

Bella laughed, then winced. "Not too hard. I'm stitched up. Could someone please just hold the baby who isn't fighting over the Ottoman Empire?"

Gia extended her hands and picked up the baby. Ana stood still.

Nonna cradled the baby with theatrical reverence and beamed, "Abraham. Big name. Old name. My grandfather had a goat named Abraham."

Ana raised an eyebrow. "My grandfather was Abraham."

Gia smiled. "So we agree. It runs in the family."

"He smells like—like-"

Gia sniffed Abi and then passed him to Ana as a peace offering.

The baby-Abraham—warm and small and real. His eyes were barely open, his fists balled in tight protest against the brightness of the world. He was wrapped in soft flannel, a blue thread embroidered along the edge—not for gender, but for protection.

Ana sniffed him and exhaled, "Bread!"

Gia nodded and sat in a chair in the corner beside Ruslan.

Ana whispered to the child, a lullaby from her mother's lips: "You came from stars, from silence, from so many broken threads stitched back together…"

Abraham blinked up at her. His hand opened and closed in the air, like he was reaching for something just beyond.

Rocco looked around and whispered. "Anyone wants grappa? I brought grappa."

"No one is giving the newborn grappa, Rocco," Bella said flatly.

He laughed. "Not for him. For us. To celebrate!"

They sat, bickered, and passed the baby like diplomats handing over a peace treaty. Somewhere between tea and diaper talk, the room filled—not with guests, but with something fuller—a thread drawn tight again.

And Ana thought, "Tosya, can you see this?"

Ana watched them—this chaotic, affectionate, ridiculous brood—and felt, for once, no urge to correct anyone. The world was loud and strange, and this child would need every ounce of love and laughter it could get.

She looked at the boy, at her hands, which now smelled of milk, bread, and hope. She looked at the mother, tired and glowing, who had once run off, then returned—twice—both times stomping in Italian heels, but the second time carrying new life. She looked at the father, who had once been all anger and absence, now steady and present, stunned into awe.

And Ana thought: "Let them baptize. Let them bicker. Let them love. He will carry all of us."

Oh, boy, and just like that, this thread—wild, frayed, defiant—was weaving again.

Chapter Sixty-Five
Bubble

They didn't sleep, but it didn't matter. The world was small now—a world of three—orbiting around a bassinet, a baby monitor, and a fridge full of things no one had the energy to cook.

Eli stood in the kitchen at 2:17 a.m., holding a bottle under hot water like it was a holy object.

"It's too hot," he muttered. "No—too cold." He shook a few drops on his wrist like he'd seen in a movie. "Now lukewarm. Like a nice banya."

Bella leaned in from the hallway, hair wild, eyes bleary. "You're warming the formula. You know that, right?"

"I'm warming it with love."

"You're overthinking it."

"You're under—sanitizing."

"Do you want to do this at 2:18 a.m.?"

Eli raised the bottle. "For you, cara mia, anything."

They fed him. They burped him. They forgot to burp him and then learned what happened when you forgot. They tried to swaddle him like the nurse had shown, but Bella's version looked like an origami, and Eli's looked like a burrito that had lost hope.

Still, Abi slept. Not always where he was supposed to, but he slept—in arms, on chests, across knees, in between the two of them in their bed. His tiny fingers curled instinctively around theirs, his eyes blinking like old light bulbs remembering how to glow.

Sometimes Bella would just stare at him.

"He looks like you," she'd whisper.

Eli would shake his head. "He looks like a baby."

"Your forehead. Look. Right there."

"That's a forehead? I thought it was just… head."

And sometimes, when the baby was finally down, they would collapse on the couch and stare at the silence.

"Do you think we're doing okay?" Bella whispered once.

Eli looked at her. "He's still alive."

"That's the bar?"

"Yes. For now. Later, we raise it."

Later meant different things to both of them. For now, they lived in a soft bubble of lullabies and sterilized pacifiers, baby wipes in every room, and the constant game of: Did you check his diaper?

They spoke in fragments, switching between languages like gears in an old car:

"Nu shto, Abi, you're not tired?"

"Ma che, he just woke up."

"Abi, zayt gezunt, don't eat the sock!"

"Don't say 'don't' so much," Bella said.

"What am I supposed to say?"

"Reframe it. Say: we chew food, not socks."

"He's six months old, not a Professor."

They were overprotective in the way only first—time parents can be. They bought five kinds of thermometers. They refused to let anyone kiss him. They panicked over every sneeze, every rash, every oddly shaped poop. Another time, Bella called the pediatrician's office three times in one day, once about a weird noise Abi made when he sneezed.

They argued, too.

Not the kind of arguments that left bruises, but the type that tested the seams—tugged at the corners of who they used to be before they became someone's parents.

"I think we should baptize him," Bella said one evening, gently and cautiously, spoon in hand, mid—dinner.

Eli didn't look up. "We're not baptizing him."

"Why not?"

"Because I don't believe in that."

"You don't believe in brit milah either."

"No," he said, putting down the fork. "But I believe in not cutting him. Or dunking him. Or labeling him before he even knows how to sit up."

She sighed. "My mama would want-"

"My mama would haunt-"

"Okay!" she snapped, and the baby started to cry. They both froze.

In the end, they did neither.

No ritual. No priest. No mohel. Just a red thread tied on a tiny wrist, a lullaby hummed in Italian, and a whispered prayer in Yiddish. They circled the crib with nervous love and sealed it with a kiss.

And despite sleepless nights, Bella flourished and glowed. Beneath the daily spit, sour milk, and squash puree, she found untamed but also tender love towards Abi. He was the reason she ran away from Eli and the reason she did come back. The love that filled her was nothing that she had ever felt before. On the nights when the time stood still, Bella would sit in the armchair beside the window and sing lullabies. And in that moment, both Bella and Abi were inseparable as only a mother and a child could be.

The days passed in small glories: his first smile (accidental), his first genuine smile (undeniable), the way he grabbed Eli's nose like a lifeline, the way he burrowed into Bella's collarbone like he belonged there.

The world was full of moments. They came like stars—some bright, some flickering, some so quick you almost missed them.

But they saw them. They remembered.

And even when the exhaustion carved valleys into their faces, even when the noise never stopped, they felt that they were invincible. They thought it would last forever.

Chapter Sixty-Six
Void

In Los Angeles, after Bella left New York, she wore her hunger well. The Eighties were roaring and howling, spilling into the glitter—filled Nineties. In the clean white halls of the museum she called hers, she carried herself like a piece of living sculpture—sharp angles softened by loud laughter, wit spilling from her as fast as champagne into tall glasses. She learned how to hold a room the way some women hold a note: effortlessly and with a hint of danger.

She had what she once wanted: walls filled with paintings that shocked and seduced, patrons who listened when she spoke about form and colour, donors who called her bella Bella as if she were a talisman, men who leaned too close at openings and women who envied the flesh of her heels. She had lovers, brief and glittering as brushstrokes. Nights spilled into mornings of wine, velvet, and arguments over art.

In the dark, Bella clawed at strangers as if touch itself could feed her. She bit their lips, arched into their weight, rode the heat until her voice was raw. Their hands were greedy, their thrusts graceless, and still she urged them on, desperate for the burn in her blood to drown the ache in her chest. They left her slick with sweat, the sheets twisted, the air thick with smoke and wine.

And always—when her body quieted—memory intruded: Eli's hand steady on her hip, his soft hands drawing her body anew. The men of Los Angeles gave her heat, but never home. She did not belong to them, the way she did with

Eli. She came alive in the moment, only to feel emptier after, her hunger sharpened by the taste of something she could never find again.

She screamed herself empty, only to lie awake after, hungrier than before, in silence. The kind that pressed against the ribs. The kind that left her staring at ceiling shadows, waiting for something that never returned. Eli had been the opposite of all this—no dazzle, no performance. Just devotion, solid and quiet as breath. Bella filled her days with brilliance, but none of it filled the hollow his absence left.

Once, in the mid—nineties, she returned to New York for Thanksgiving. The subway clattered beneath her, and there—across the car—were Ana and Tosya, bundled in coats, arms heavy with parcels. Their heads bent together, tired but purposeful, they carried food to a church basement that smelled of boiled potatoes and hope.

Bella's throat closed. She wanted to call out, to press through the crowd, to say her name, to remind them she still existed. But she didn't. She let the train carry her in the opposite direction, heart pounding like a drum of regret. They did not notice her. She saw them. That was enough to shatter, to feel the ache and the void. When the doors opened, she stumbled out, breathless, her heart tearing itself apart, and ran home.

The Caruso house at Thanksgiving was chaos, as always—voices ricocheting off the walls, pots clattering, the smell of garlic and turkey fighting for dominance. Gia shouted over Nonna about the stuffing, Rocco banged his glass with a spoon until someone passed the wine, and he tried to carve the bird while everyone criticized his technique.

Bella swept in like she always did, her heels clicking, her scarf tossed over her shoulder, and a little too much lipstick.

She let them kiss her cheeks, let them tell her she looked like a movie star, then slid into her chair with the confidence of someone who had escaped and made something of herself.

"You in the papers again?" Rocco said, pouring wine too full. "My Bella, my girl, the art queen of Los Angeles."

"Curator," Bella corrected, her smile sharp. "Not queen. Queens sit around waiting for crowns. I make things happen."

Rocco nodded and raised his glass. "To Bella—she wanted it, and she got it."

But Gia's voice cut through the laughter, blunt as always: "You got what you wanted, figlia. But you're not thankful for it. You're not happy."

The table quieted just enough to make the words sting.

Bella's laugh came too loud, too brittle. "What do you want me to be? A housewife in Queens? I'm building something real."

"You let the good one go," Gia said, soft this time, almost tender.

Bella's hand froze on her glass. For a moment, the clamour of the Caruso house dulled, and all she could hear was her own pulse hammering in her ears. She raised her glass anyway, flashing a grin too bright, talking too fast, drowning the ache. The family roared back to life around her-Rocco telling a joke, Nonna shouting at the turkey—but the words had already sunk their teeth in. She could change cities, men, and the art on her walls, but she could not change that truth.

That night, she found herself in her childhood room. The wallpaper had faded, and the bed was too small. Bella pressed her face into the pillow and cried like a girl again because, for all her lovers and all her success, she knew her mother was right.

She got up and grabbed a phone. With trembling fingers, she dialled his number. She listened to the ring, her pulse racing. There was a click on the other end—someone lifting the receiver. She hung up before a voice came through. She pressed her forehead to the phone, whispering into silence. The museum, the lovers, the laughter, the city—all of it dissolved into the ache of one truth: she had built her life around freedom, but every breath still missed him.

Bella continued in her loud and bright world, a collage of openings, empty apartments, enormous catalogues, and sleek wine glasses. Her hunger never dimmed, but nothing fed it. She had chosen brilliance over devotion, freedom over tether. And still—every night, when the whispers faded—the void remained. Until they met again.

Chapter Sixty-Seven
Y2K (Y 2 Killed?)

Ana was the one who insisted they go.

"Go," she said, waving them off like she had somewhere else to be. "You're still young. He's asleep. I'll feed him if he wakes. Just go—be together. Be stupid. Be in love."

Bella hesitated on the threshold, her coat half on, hair pinned back the way she now wore it, then turned back toward the crib. "He just fell asleep," she said.

Eli stepped behind her, wrapped his arms around her and whispered, "He'll still be asleep when we get back. Let's live a little."

Ruslan handed them their scarves like a valet. "I will see you next year, no, next century, wait, next millenium," he grinned. "But If the world ends tonight, I want to see it as well."

"Then we will take the cab," Eli said, "Go and celebrate it with Misha!"

And so they went. Dressed too lightly for the snow, too happily for the time.

The city shimmered, with lights strung across avenues, every window spilling laughter, and every street alive with people in cheap sequins and overpriced shoes. Even the sky looked festive, bruised with pink and gold.

They arrived at the party—some gallery downtown, all concrete and mirrors—and for a while, it felt like something from a forgotten decade. Music from another time. Eli didn't know half the people; Bella didn't care. She was in his lap on a low velvet couch, tracing the line of his collarbone with her finger, whispering little nothings that made him blush and swallow hard.

They danced like lovers with a secret—her dress slipping off her shoulder, his hands a little too low on her back. She kissed him beneath the coloured lights, slow, indulgent, as if tasting every part of the life they'd fought for.

He pressed his forehead to hers and murmured, "You're my whole calendar now."

"Good," she said, biting his lip gently. "Then mark me down for all year, no, the whole century and maybe even millennium!"

At one point, a woman in a silver dress leaned in and asked, "You two married?"

Bella nodded. "Oh, yes," she said. "Shotgun wedding. The baby just turned six months."

Eli smirked. "I insisted."

The lady smiled and whispered, "You have a spark! Keep it burning!"

They laughed and kissed, and then the countdown began.

Ten. Nine. Eight…

Bella gripped his lapel. "Next year," she whispered, "Rome."

"And Paris!" he said.

Three. Two. One—

Midnight.

The room roared. Champagne spilled. People screamed, kissed, laughed, and clapped because the lights didn't flicker, and the world didn't end.

Not yet.

And when the party was over, they hailed a cab. It was quiet. Bella rested her head on Eli's shoulder, her lipstick now mostly his.

Snow fell like ash. The world was new and so still.

He kissed her once. Then again. She giggled and pressed her cold nose to his cheek.

The truck's lights came suddenly, too close, too fast.

Their lips were still touching when the world went white.

Blood spread on the asphalt and froze—red threads snaking across the black glass of the street mixed with the colourful serpentine streamers. The blood glittered under the headlights, bright and obscene, as if it belonged to some tapestry now torn open at the seam.

Somewhere far away, a siren wailed—shrill, rising.

And in the apartment above the city, Ana, holding a cup of tea, looked toward the window as her hand trembled. Something ancient, bone—deep, stirred in her. The thread tugged.

Her heart sank. As if she already knew.

The year turned, the decade, the century, the millennium. But so did the cab. The world went on. But nothing would ever be the same.

Chapter Sixty-Eight
Betrayal

The knock came just after dawn. Not frantic. Not hesitant. Just… final. Ana already knew. Somehow, before the sound even echoed, she knew. She opened the door slowly. Two officers stood there—solemn, clipped, soaked in someone else's sorrow. She did not ask which one.

She simply said, "Both?"

They nodded.

At the morgue, the lights were too bright. Gia was wailing in Italian, her voice scraping the white walls. Rocco stood like a man cut in half, his hands trembling as he signed the papers.

"I told her not to go!" Gia shouted. "Not on New Year's! Not in this weather!"

"They took a cab, Gia," Ana muttered. "What do you want? For the earth to stand still while they fell in love again?"

"Don't talk to me like that! She was my daughter!"

"He was my son." Ana's voice cracked like glass.

The attendant opened the drawer. Bella first. Then Eli. Pale. Frozen. Their hands still bore glitter from the party.

Gia collapsed into Rocco. Ana had nobody; she did not cry. Her body felt like iron—too rusted to bend.

Later, they fought. Quietly but viciously. In the hallway. Over where to bury them.

"They'll have a proper Mass," Gia snapped. "A priest. Her Nonna would-"

"She'll be beside her husband," Ana hissed. "My son will not rot under a cross he didn't believe in."

Gia's eyes narrowed. "So you want to bury them both like strangers?"

"No," Ana whispered. "I want to bury them beside each other like family. My, your family. Where David and Tosya are."

A long silence. Then Rocco, stunned and broken, simply said, "Fine."

And it was done.

The funeral was sparse. Too fast. Too cold. New Year's frost on the ground, the kind that eats through boots and hope alike.

But this time, there was no shiva. Ana refused it. No mirrors covered, no low chairs, no candles burning.

She did not want the rabbi's voice or strangers' hands on her back, saying, "May their memory be a blessing."

She did not want blessings. She did not want God. She did not want to sit for seven days and pretend that grief could be measured and scheduled. She wanted silence. She wanted to sit in it. Let the casseroles pile up at the door. Let the community whisper. She stayed inside, alone, her fists clenched around the silence like it was the only thing that hadn't betrayed her. She didn't speak. Her voice had died with them.

That night after the burial, she returned home. The silence clung to the walls. Ruslan had stayed with the baby.

"He didn't wake," he said gently.

Ana only nodded. Ruslan left quietly.

She made tea, pouring it too hot. She sat at the table and stared into the steam until her hands began to shake. Then, finally, she broke. She howled—not cried—howled—like something ancient, something from the desert or the woods. She screamed at God, Bella, Eli, the door, the walls, and the window. She clawed at the rug and tore a dish towel in half.

Her voice cracked: "Why… why… why did you give them back to me just to rip them away again?"

The kettle clicked off. She didn't hear it.

Then—a cry. A baby's cry. High. Piercing. Unbearably alive.

Ana froze. Her face twisted. For a moment—just a flash—she hated him. Hated that he had lived when they had not. Hated the sound of him, the weight of him, the smell of him, the shape of him. She walked to his crib, slow and stiff as a ghost. Abraham flailed, his face blotched with tears.

"I can't do this," she whispered.

He cried harder. He didn't care. And then—something inside her cracked open. She reached in. Picked him up. Pressed him against her chest. Her heart beat against his, fast and terrified. She rocked him. Rocked and rocked. Brought him to the armchair and sat there as if time had stopped. And then, her voice hoarse and low, she began to sing. A lullaby. The same one she sang to Roza.

The same one she sang to Eli, "Oyfn pripetshik brent a fayerl…" Then, more quietly: "Spi, moye dytya…"-sleep, my child…

A thread. Thin. Trembling. Unbroken. Life, somehow, insisted on continuing. And so she held him. Sang to him. Let the red thread wind its way through one more night.

Chapter Sixty-Nine
Baba

It was a week after the funeral.

Ana's apartment was hushed and bright—full of clean lines, polished wood, quiet money. The kind of silence that didn't ask for conversation. It demanded composure.

Abi was asleep in his pram, pacifier bobbing gently. Six months old. Blissfully unaware.

Gia was not unaware.

"I won't let you just take him," she said, standing too straight, arms folded. "He's not a painting."

"I didn't take him, they all live… lived here," Ana said from her armchair, her voice calm. "He's been here all this time, and this last week since…"

"That's because I let it be," Gia snapped. "We were all mourning. We needed time. But it's been a week. I'm his Nonna."

"And I am his Baba. And I will not hand him back like luggage after a layover."

Gia scoffed. "Is this because you have the bigger place? The elevator? The art on the walls? You think he needs a view of the skyline?"

"I think he needs quiet. Predictability. And you, Gia, you have three other grandchildren, and you will have more! I will have—and have had—only one."

That landed like a stone.

Gia blinked. "Don't you throw that at me like it's some punishment."

"I'm not punishing anyone. I'm trying to give him, us, a home."

"You think I can't give him one?"

"I think," Ana said, softly but firmly, "that this is the right choice. Not because I'm rich. Because I'm ready. You're still grieving Bella."

"And you're not?"

"I've been grieving longer than you think."

There was a long pause.

"I bathed her when she was a baby," Gia whispered. "Her first fever, it was me. I sat with her all night. Her communion, her scraped knees, her fights with the nuns and her brothers…"

Gia just stopped as the silent tears consumed her. Ana didn't say a word, and the silence now felt biblical.

Rocco, who'd been sitting on the couch, slouching but in a rare suit, finally spoke. His voice was gentle but steady: "Enough."

They turned to him.

"She is not the enemy, Gia," he said. "And neither are you, Ana. But if you make this about pride, you will both lose."

"I'm not trying to win," Ana said, her voice thick now. "I just—he's all I have. I want him to grow up with someone who's already buried too many people to let anything happen to him."

Gia stared at her: "And what do I get?"

Ana swallowed. "Sundays. Always. Holidays. Any time you want."

"No appointments?"

"No appointments."

"I want a key."

"You can have two!"

Rocco extended his hand as if asking Ana to stop, "We don't need a key. We just want Abi and you in our lives."

Gia sank onto the couch, fur coat still on. "He'll call me Nonna."

"He will!"

"And when he asks what happened to his parents?"

Ana looked at the sleeping child. " We would tell him they were light, are light, they are stars, his guiding stars."

Gia wiped her eyes with the back of her hand. "You better not mess this up."

"I won't," Ana said.

Rocco stood. "It's settled."

Gia nodded, almost regal in defeat. "He lives with you. Not because you're rich. Because it's the right choice."

Ana nodded, her voice nearly breaking. "Thank you."

Abi stirred in his sleep. Ana stood, lifted him gently, and kissed his forehead. He smelled of milk and something sweet, like safety.

Gia watched, then sighed. "Don't dress him like an old man. He's a baby, not a Professor."

Rocco grinned. "And don't forget his pasta on Sundays."

Ana, without smiling, replied, "He'll be waiting."

And just like that, a fragile truce was drawn. Not perfect. But real. Like family.

Chapter Seventy
Chauffeur

It began, like most things, with inertia. After the funeral, no one really moved. Or breathed. Or changed their socks unless absolutely necessary. Ana had no intention of going anywhere. But the baby needed air, and the apartment, with its thick silence and perfect light, had started to feel like a mausoleum.

So one morning, without asking, Ruslan wheeled the pram outside.

Ana noticed only because her tea had gone quiet. She found herself looking out the window like Baba Yaga, the old witch in a Russian folktale. Although she was more refined than her, she had the same bitterness and incurable heartache.

By the third morning, he waited by the kitchen door.

"You should come," he said gently. "We walk past the old woman with the dogs. She stares at us every time."

And so, they began to walk together. Sometimes.

It wasn't what either of them planned. Ruslan was supposed to be the driver. A shadow. A helper. But Ana didn't want a stranger changing diapers and pretending not to flinch when Abi screamed like a wounded goat. She didn't want someone contemplating between how to swaddle a Jewish—Italian miracle baby or feel sorry for the poor orphan, well, not really poor, but still an orphan.

No. Ruslan had known Bella. Had listened to Eli. Had drunk Tosya's tea and nodded politely through her long, incoherent stories in broken English, Soviet Russian, and village Ukrainian. He was, without trying, the last thread. He knew who they had been—which meant he understood who was gone and who remained.

And somehow, the man who once flinched at boys—and loud noises in general—began to hum lullabies under his breath. He carried the diaper bag like a briefcase. He navigated teething gel and pacifier preferences with the precision of a Swiss engineer.

"Your manny used to drive a Rolls-Royce and now-Peg Perego?" a nosy neighbour said, eyes wide as she rode the elevator with Ana.

Ana blinked. "Still a chauffeur," she said flatly.

"But he watches the baby…"

Ana kept silent.

The lady with the dogs tried to be subtler.

"Is he…" she murmured, leaning close. "You know. That way."

Ana didn't blink. "Kind? Loving? The one person who hasn't disappointed me this year?"

The woman flushed. "No, I just meant-"

"You meant something small," Ana said, pressing the elevator button with finality. "I don't have time for small."

Tosya, had she been there, would've handled it differently. She would've said something along the lines of that being stupid was a bigger sin.

Then, one morning, while Ruslan buckled Abi into the stroller, he muttered, "Thank God he survived."

Ana froze. The air in the room thinned.

"What God?" she said.

Ruslan turned.

"Yours? Mine? The God who punishes children and leaves old women to cry over tiny shoes?"

"Ana…"

"No. If God were a woman, she would've cared."

They stood there, the baby humming quietly between them, like a metronome.

"I only just started to believe again," Ruslan said softly.

"And I just stopped."

They didn't speak about it again. But he brought her tea that night without asking how she liked it. And she didn't complain when he used the wrong cup.

They fell into a rhythm. A strange, beautiful rhythm.

Ruslan took Abi to Nonna's house in Baba's Rolls-Royce. They returned with pasta sauce on both of their clothes. He brought him to the Russian grocery, where the old ladies pinched the baby's cheeks and declared him strong like a soldier. At the park, teenagers whispered that the "hot dad" was too young—and possibly gay—and why was his mother there?

"Not his mother," Ana corrected one of them. "Baby's Baba."

It was on a spring morning—not too bright, not too cold—that Abi, drooling and flapping his arms like a disgruntled pigeon, little holub, reached for Ana and said it for the first time: "Baba."

She stopped breathing. Ruslan looked up. Her hands shook.

"Bozhe moi," she whispered.

And smiled. Just a little. Just enough. Maybe she was beginning to forgive her God. Or maybe, she thought, some things were too precious to explain.

Chapter Seventy-One
Before and After

Before, there was silence. Not the peaceful kind. The kind that screams through walls. The kind that lives in the bones, long after the bruises fade.

Before, he was a boy with soft hands and a gentle voice that didn't match his name. A boy who flinched too easily. Who folded his limbs small so no one would notice. Who had once believed that being quiet could make you invisible—or safe.

That belief didn't survive the orphanage.

He was thirteen. A war orphan. A name on a list. Sent to a building with gray walls and boys twice his size. There were no lullabies in Perm. Only fists. And laughter that came with teeth. They took everything. His body. His language. His God. And when he stopped crying, they called him strong.

And five years later, Ruslan stood on the New York subway platform, the cold pressing into his bones like a warning. He had a paper cup of tea from a kiosk. It had gone cold. He didn't remember buying it. The train was coming—a silver streak that promised an end. The noise filled his ears, but inside, everything was empty.

He thought of the war, the nights when gunfire replaced lullabies, and the world burned around him. He thought of the faces lost, the silence that followed—deeper than any night. He thought of a boy who once dreamed of peace and a life unbroken.

The train thundered toward him like an answer. His feet didn't move. He waited—maybe for a sign, maybe just for something louder than his own thoughts. The train opened its doors and swallowed him; he was still breathing, but not truly alive. He curled into the seat in the corner, in his parka, half asleep and half dead.

Then a voice—soft, stubborn—cut through. And everything shifted. The rails thrummed like a heartbeat, steady and rising—a rhythm that carried him toward everything he did not yet know.

He became a chauffeur, and he learned how to drive and take care of the car. Then, he learned how to take care of the baby, boil bottles, fold onesies, and tell the difference between Abi's tired cry and his hungry one. He learned which stroller wheels stuck on the curb, which brand of wipes didn't make the baby rashy, and that Ana liked her tea black, steeped too long, with a lemon slice she never actually used.

He never spoke of the train. Ana never asked.

Some mornings, he watched Abi sleep and thought, How fragile you are. And still… how sure of love. He couldn't remember ever being that sure. But he could carry it forward for someone else.

He had grown taller, or maybe just more solid. People looked at him differently now—with softness, sometimes with trust.

The same man who once avoided mirrors now studied the baby's reflection in the hallway glass, adjusting the carrier strap with practiced care. His hands, which had once curled into fists at night, now fit perfectly around a bottle, a teething toy, a tiny sock.

Once, Ana told him, "You're the only human I trust with him."

He hadn't known what to say. He just nodded. He didn't need more than that.

But shadows were still there. At night, he woke with fists clenched, breath tight. But there was also light—in the window, on the baby's cheeks, in the steam from the tea Ana made him without asking, Misha's potato salad, their quiet apartment with loud art and music.

He wasn't healed. He didn't believe in that word. But he had stopped disappearing. He had a key. A house. A stroller to push. A child who reached for him with sticky fingers and unconditional faith. A woman who didn't speak in compliments but left the food to take home to Misha. A boyfriend who only had eyes and heart for him. They all spoke one language, and, no, it was not Russian, but a language of hope, love, and acceptance.

He hadn't become someone else. Just… more of who he was, without shame.

That spring morning, when Abi called Ana "Baba", Ruslan had looked up sharply, heart stuttering like he'd heard a prayer said right. Ana's eyes filled. Just a little. And Ruslan smiled. Not wide. Not all the way.

Light spilled across the worn table where two cups waited. Ruslan watched Misha laugh—small, imperfect, but real. The weight inside him was still there, but softer now, worn down by the steady rhythm of days lived side by side.

He reached for Misha's hand, fingers trembling.

"No promises," he whispered. "Just today."

And that was enough. He had a family to be with, to love, and to take care of.

Chapter Seventy-Two
Broken

Abi was not raised. He was cultivated. By age six, he spoke five languages and read in two of them. There were tutors for French, Hebrew, Russian, Italian, and one exhausted young man from Oxford who attempted to teach him English grammar but left crying after Ana corrected his syntax.

"No grandson of mine will be illiterate," Ana had declared.

"He's five," Ruslan had whispered.

"Five is practically six," Ana snapped. "And six is nearly ten, and ten is almost too late."

There were classical music lessons. (Violin—short-lived, as he did not have the talent for it like his dad. Piano—better.) There were daily reading sessions of Chekhov, Homer (the Greek one), and something called Pinocchio and Buratino, about a wooden boy with a long nose who, if he told a lie, his nose would grow longer.

Tosya would've said, "Of course, Ana, you have to read to him about the big nose as if he should have the constant reminder that he is blessed with one."

And every Sunday, like a clock, they went to see Nonna and Nonno in Baba's Rolls-Royce. The whole Caruso clan, loud, tomato—scented, full of opinions and unsolicited advice, was there. Rocco taught Abi how to fix a leaky faucet. Gia showed him how to taste sauce like a critic and never to trust a man or a woman who doesn't like garlic.

Abi brought his books and his drawings.

"You know what I had at his age?" Rocco muttered, sipping espresso. "A wrench. And a basement. That's it."

Gia shushed him. "So what? Let the boy learn. He will be a Professor one day!"

Rocco said, "At least it is not from our side."

Gia reacted, "I have a PhD in pasta, lasagna, and cannoli. It's a different kind of genius. And don't forget, Bella did graduate from Columbia."

They stopped bickering and looked at each other. The grief was still there—quieter now, but no less sharp.

And it was Ruslan who now became a permanent fixture.

He ironed Abi's tiny shirts, braided wild science projects out of sticks and glue, and built Lego castles with moats, towers, and catapults that actually worked.

They had a game: Sir Abi and the Knight of the North. Abi wielded a plastic sword with dramatic flair. Ruslan wore a dish towel as a cape. Their enemies were dragons, poor grammar, and bad dreams.

Something shifted in Ruslan during those moments of shared innocent laughter, as if the years at the detskii dom—that cold Perm orphanage with its thin soup and thick fist of the boys—finally thawed. He was still quiet, still flinched at fireworks and door slams, but with Abi, he laughed. He let his guard down. He smiled.

And then—slowly, softly-Abi started changing. He began to nap longer. Play less.

He would hold his chest sometimes and say, "It feels tight."

Ana waved it off at first. "Growing pains."

But then his teachers began to mention that he was tired in the afternoons. He didn't run as much and winced when they walked to the library.

Ruslan noticed. He watched Abi like a soldier on night watch. Counted his breaths. Tracked his naps. Brought it up to Ana quietly, then more urgently.

Ana didn't want to hear it. "He's fine," she insisted. "He just reads too much. He's as delicate as his father was. Maybe take him to the park more often. Fresh air and some exercise will cure anything!"

But her fingers trembled when she tied his shoelaces. She began watching him like Tosya once watched Eli—as if waiting for a shadow to fall.

The day it happened, the sky was so blue it felt like an insult.

Abi had been playing with his knight set when he suddenly clutched his chest and gasped—a sound like a baby bird hitting glass.

He couldn't breathe.

His tiny body arched. His hands fluttered like broken wings.

"My heart," he said. "It's flying."

Ana froze. Ruslan moved. No hesitation. No words. He wrapped the boy in a blanket and shouted for the keys. They didn't take an ambulance. They took the Rolls-Royce. Baba's Rolls-Royce. Because some part of Ana—stubborn and illogical—believed it might protect them, driving in the ambulance felt like he would not make it. Because every time the ambulance came for someone she loved, it never brought them back.

Abi lay in the backseat, pale and fluttering. Ana held his hand, muttering every prayer she could remember, in every language she knew. Ruslan drove like the city belonged to him. Red lights, sirens, nothing mattered. The streets parted. Or maybe they didn't. The lights stretched their threads as a spider web, and the car felt like a fly trying to avoid being caught.

All Ana could hear was the sound of Abi's breath and his fleeting heart. And then—the chaos that followed. And then—the chaos swallowed them. Fluorescent lights. Sliding doors. The blur of gurneys and gloves. The hospital—that cold, humming black hole—pulled them in without mercy. White coats, white hallways, and white rooms. Where the air smelled like endings. Where time stretched and then snapped, where she had once lost a husband, then a friend and down below it had housed Abi's parents in the silver boxes for one final night.

And now-Abi was here. Her little pigeon, her holub, with the wings that were pulling him down and the heart that was skipping a bit.

Chapter Seventy-Three
Faith-Vera

Hospitals were never quiet. They hummed—with machines, footsteps, and the almost audible static of breath held too long. The hospital wing was newer than Ana remembered—all muted pastels and quiet lighting, an attempt at mercy. But she could still hear the hum beneath the walls. Some rooms carry memories like mildew.

She sat in the waiting area with her back straight, lips pressed, and handbag perched on her knees like a visitor. She didn't tell anyone that she had paid for this wing—anonymously, years ago, when a building needed new bodies and she had too many ghosts. It was just the sort of thing she did. Quietly. Out of grief. Out of love. Out of something older than both. She paid the tuition for refugees who wanted to attend college and provided grants to musicians and artists, future doctors, and nurses.

Tosya always said, "Spend while living and on people, as there are no pockets on a coffin."

Now she sat in its silence, the air thick with the smell of coffee and disinfectant. Gia paced like a metronome. Rocco, bless him, kept trying to fix the coffee machine that was taking the coins but not spitting out the coffee. No tools, no luck. Just that instinct—if something is broken, maybe he can put it back.

Ruslan hadn't said a word. He sat beside Ana, a hand on her arm, as if trying to hold their world steady.

The door opened with a quiet click. A doctor stepped in—around mid—thirties, slight, sharp—eyed, with curly black hair. She looked familiar before she spoke.

"Ana," she said gently, "It's been a long time."

Something inside Ana startled, and she squinted. The voice was older and more precise, but the eyes were still quiet—unblinking.

"Vera?"

The doctor nodded once. "Dr. Verahimana now," she said. "But you can still call me Vera."

There was silence, then a long look and as if in a code that only two of them could understand, Dr. Vera said, "Some debts find their way. Old country rules."

Ana smiled and nodded, "Dr. Vera?"

The next hours unravelled in slow turns. Tests. Monitors. Consultations. The heart was failing, they said, delicately. It was the sort of defect that hides until it doesn't. A genetic trace, passed down like a story no one meant to tell.

"There's a very small window," Vera explained. "We've entered it."

The problem wasn't the surgery. The problem was the match. The child's blood and markers were too particular and too rare. Time was both an enemy and a ticking bomb. And hope—well, hope was a hallway. You walk it until it runs out.

"A miracle," said Dr. Vera, hands folded. "That's what it would take."

Ana hated the word "miracle". It required hope. It required faith.

Gia exclaimed. "I will light every candle in Brooklyn."

Rocco said as a matter of fact, "He's a Caruso, he'll fight."

And for the first time in years, in her head, Ana started praying in all the languages that she knew, to the God that she thought had forgotten her.

Rocco rubbed his hands together. "Is it… is it like plumbing?" he asked, blinking hard. "You swap out the part?"

"More or less," Dr. Vera smiled. "But it has to be the right part."

And then came the waiting. One day. Two. Four. The days bled into weeks. The hospital became a second skin. Gia and Rocco brought food. Ana barely touched hers.

Ruslan stayed, reading books, colouring pages, and making shadow Knights and Kings on the wall to keep Abi entertained. Ruslan didn't speak much to anyone else but Abi. He slept in a chair, shoes off, legs curled under like a stork. He braided paper cranes from hospital forms. He whispered stories of a Knight who slept to gather strength for the final battle.

Abi mostly stayed in his bed, pale as bone, a bird wrapped in blankets, his heart labouring under his ribs like it had somewhere else it needed to be. Machines blinked gently around him like worried mothers.

The call came when they lost count. Vera rushed into the waiting room with her coat still on.

"There's a donor," she said, voice tight. "A girl. From Russia. Car crash. A small hospital. One of the nurses remembered a program. Called us herself."

She looked at Ana. "It's a match. Blood, tissue, everything. If the heart survives the flight, we go."

No one spoke. Rocco crossed himself. Gia exhaled something like a prayer in Italian and burst into tears. Ruslan put a hand to his face and didn't move.

Ana just closed her eyes.

Vera stepped closer, crouched in front of her like a daughter might.

"I stitch hearts now," she said. "And I'll do my best with his."

For the first time in days, Ana allowed herself to lean—not much, just a few degrees—into someone else.

But it was not so simple.

Dr. Vera didn't promise miracles. "Just a chance," she said. "And sometimes that's enough."

Ana paid for the transport and the team. The heart was en route. It would arrive by dawn. And when it did—a tiny, strong heart that had loved dolls and songs and pigtails-Dr. Vera stood at the table like a priest at the altar. She would try. That's all she ever did. Try to keep one more heart from breaking. Try to stitch two lives into one body.

Chapter Seventy-Four
Gifted

Abi came home with a new heart and a new attitude. Now he stayed three days at Nonna's and four at Baba's. It was a diplomatic arrangement, established over much negotiation (and one dramatic episode involving a missing stuffed giraffe and a solemn vote). It allowed everyone a chance to hover and overfeed, and it gave Abi an escape route whenever one side got too sentimental.

"Don't carry the bag, Baba," he said solemnly to Ana. "You're too old. Your bones are made of breadsticks."

Ana raised an eyebrow. "They're steel, actually."

He nodded. "Stale steel," and then giggled so hard he got the hiccups.

In the end, Ruslan carried the bag, the flowers, and the stuffed animal collection that had somehow multiplied during the hospital stay, mostly thanks to Gia, who insisted, "Every day alive is another reason for a bear."

At Carusos, Nonno Rocco installed a bell by Abi's bed. "If you need anything, you ring, okay?"

Abi rang it thirty—two times the first night.

"I need grapes."

"I need to test the bell."

"I need to tell you something important: I saw a ghost."

By the next morning, the bell had mysteriously disappeared. Rocco claimed plumbing issues.

Nonna Gia made chicken cutlets in the shape of hearts. "For strength," she said, tearing basil like a prayer.

She hovered. She prayed over his pasta. She snuck holy water into his apple juice.

And then, without warning, she took him to church and had him baptized.

"For protection," she whispered to the priest.

"You'll thank me when you're older," Gia told Abi, dabbing his forehead with a handkerchief that smelled like sugar and oregano all at the same time. "You're covered now. No loopholes."

Abi came home to Baba Ana, smugly talking about sacramental water. "I'm triple now," he said. I'm Jewish, Catholic, and sprinkled."

Ana nearly dropped her teacup. "Bozhe moi."

One afternoon, Ana walked into Abi's room and caught him reading one of Eli's old books, a thick Russian novel with too many footnotes.

"Why that one?" she asked.

Abi shrugged. "I like how sad it is."

Ana smiled faintly. "He did too."

Abi looked up. "I think he'd like me."

Ana touched his hair. "He'd be scared of how much."

And Ruslan continued to be his quiet shadow. He drove him to appointments. He peeled apples the way Abi liked—one long curling ribbon. He carried books in the glove compartment. Sometimes, Abi fell asleep in the backseat while Ruslan played old Soviet lullabies softly through the speakers.

They had a rhythm now. A boy and a man who knew too much, pretending not to.

At night, Abi left notes under Gia's pillow.

One said, "I think I'm going to live forever."

Another: "Please don't ever make lentils again. They give me flatulence. "

Hid Gia's reading glasses in the freezer. Rearranged the magnets on the fridge to spell out "NO RAPINI EVER."

Sometimes Ana would hear the laughter echoing down the hallway, and for half a second, she expected to hear Tosya's voice call out, "He's too smart, that one. Hide all your money and silver."

But they caught on.

"You forget," Ana said, sipping tea. "I raised your father."

"I raised your uncles and your mother," added Gia.

Rocco nodded.

And so it went—days filled with soup and stories and puzzles and mischief. They lived around him, orbiting gently, not too close, not too far. The heart beat on. The stitches held. The blood remembered what it meant to move forward.

One Saturday morning, Ana stood in front of the mirror. She looked at her long silver hair streaming down her back. She grabbed it in a ponytail and cut it clean with one steady hand. She didn't blink as she dropped it in the waist basket. Then she took a long breath and stood tall as if the weight of the losses had lifted.

Then she called Abi. "Come, we have somewhere to go."

"To show off you new hairdo?" Aby asked.

"To show you who you are!" Ana said.

Abi put on his favourite shirt with the stars and a bow tie. Ruslan fixed the buttons on his coat. He took it seriously.

"No car today, Ruslan," Ana said, "We will walk."

And they walked to the synagogue together. The same one where Ana had once waited for Vera. The same one where ghosts sat on the benches, polite and quiet.

When they reached the door, Ana paused. "You know, your Nonna Gia had baptized you already."

"Yes," Abi said. "But it's fine. I read online that God has room."

Ana smiled. "And what do you think?"

"I think," said Abi, "if I got a second heart, maybe I'm meant to be two people."

"Who are they?"

"One who listens," he said. "And one who remembers."

Ana touched his cheek. "That's enough."

They walked inside. The air smelled of wood polish and memory. Light fell in dusty rays through the stained glass.

And somewhere behind them, in the street, a breeze stirred. Not a miracle. Just breathe. Just life. The kind you don't ask for. The kind you're given.

A gift.

Chapter Seventy-Five
Drive

The morning had that peculiar autumn stillness—like the city had been tucked under a thin veil. Ana dressed with care. No brooch. No scarf. She just had a soft black coat and black gloves, which she hadn't worn since Eli's and Bella's funeral. She brushed her hair—short now, salt—white and freshly cut—then checked on Abi again, even though he was already pulling on his little dress shoes in the hallway.

"Do I look okay?" he asked, serious as a groom.

"You look like someone who's been through everything," she said, smoothing his collar. "And still came out kind."

Today, they were driving to meet the family of the little girl whose heart now beat in Abi's chest.

Ruslan waited downstairs. When Ana and Abi came out, he opened the door of the Rolls-Royce and bowed slightly.

"Your chariot, Baba," he said with a smirk.

"Yaga," Abi whispered and climbed in. He was dressed in his good pants and a white shirt, which he had already wrinkled by lying across the rug and claiming he was too nervous to move. In his pocket, he held a drawing he'd made—of a sunflower with snowflakes instead of seeds.

Ana rolled her eyes but smiled. She sat beside Abi. The door shut with a satisfying thunk, the car purring to life as they pulled into the street. Outside, the city bustled, but inside was quiet. A hush broken only by the occasional squeak of leather or a sigh from Abi.

"Do you think they'll look like her?" he asked.

Ana didn't answer at first. "They'll look like people who lost someone they loved."

Ruslan's eyes flicked between the road and the rearview mirror. His silence was its own kind of prayer.

Ana stared out the tinted window, the streets sliding by in soft autumn light. It was the same hue as that morning months ago when everything changed. Her reflection shimmered faintly in the glass: her face older now, lined with time and memory, but steady. Ana sat back, and memory rose uninvited.

Vasyl and Halyna, Yitzhak and Miriam, Malka, her girls—the ghosts from an ancient past. David in the armchair by the window, newspaper folded, peering at Eli like he was made of light, teaching him how to tie a tie, reading Torah together. Eli and Bella, at the City Hall, signing the marriage papers. Tosya, hunched over a bowl of pelmeni, muttering that no child should be this skinny. And Roza, that first rose. The girl with the scar. Her daughter. Time stacked oddly in her. Whole decades existed in a single breath.

"I wonder if they'll cry," Abi said quietly.

"They might," Ana said. "Or they might just sit. Sometimes grief makes people very still."

He turned toward her, suddenly aworried. "What if I cry?"

"Then you'll be the bravest one in the room," she said.

Outside, the skyline shifted. The hospital was near. Ana could feel the pull of it—the way time had folded there. She remembered the sterile light, the echoing corridors, and the shattering quiet of the moment when everything could have ended—again.

Abi's hand reached for Ana's.

"I don't know what to say," he whispered.

"You don't have to say anything," she said. "Just be real. That's more than most people ever are."

The car slowed.

"Almost there," Ruslan murmured.

Abi looked out the window. "Do you think they'll like me?"

Ana squeezed his hand. "They'll see you. That's enough."

Ana looked at him—really looked.

This boy. This thread of every life she had ever touched. Of Vasyl, Roza, David, Eli and Bella. Of all she had loved and lost. He was their echo. And their beginning.

The Rolls-Royce turned the corner, and the hospital entrance came into view. Somewhere inside, the past and future were about to meet. Ana closed her eyes, then opened them again.

"Ready?" she asked.

He nodded, then pulled the drawing from his pocket. Folded once, neatly. He held it in both hands, "As I'll ever be."

The door opened, and they stepped into the light. The air was sharper, cleaner, and expectant here.

Ruslan stood by the door, eyes down, hands respectfully clasped. He would wait. That was his way.

"Go," she said. "Be light."

Abi took a deep breath. The new heart inside him beat quietly and strongly. It belonged to a girl who dreamed of snow, maybe sunflowers, maybe something else entirely.

He walked forward, and Ana walked beside him. There were no words yet—just footsteps toward the family who had given everything. And in the hush before greeting, Ana felt it—the ache, the gratitude, the old country rule: What's offered in blood must be carried with love. And so they carried it— All of it.

Chapter Seventy-Six
Home

They waited in the quiet room the hospital had offered—not sterile, not warm. A square table, four chairs and a couch. A vase with fake peonies. The kind of space made for life's most impossible moments.

Abi clutched Ana's hand tightly, his small fingers digging in. He had insisted on wearing his blazer again, even though it made him itchy. His shoes tapped the floor rhythmically. Thump. Thump. Thump. A drummer's heartbeat.

Ruslan stood near the door, arms crossed, gaze steady. If needed, he would move mountains.

Then the door opened.

A young woman stepped in first—early thirties maybe, pale, grief—shadowed. Her face looked familiar; the stubborn dark brown curls were tied in a high ponytail. Then a man, older, tall, with hollowed eyes. And behind them—

An older woman in her sixties, with brown eyes and grey hair in a bun, walked into the room. Her coat was too large, but her posture had a certain stubborn dignity. Her face was lined but not hardened. She moved with quiet self—possession, her eyes scanning the room. Something familiar, older Halyna, the features were unmistakable.

Then she looked up, straight at Ana, and Ana gasped. A faint but unmistakable scar crossed the woman's forehead—a child's wound—a mother's memory.

"Roza," Ana got up and whispered. Her knees gave way slightly, but Ruslan was there, like always, catching her.

The woman froze.

"How…?" Ana reached forward, hands trembling, eyes wide with something deeper than shock. "How is it you? I buried you. I saw your grave-"

"I-" the woman began, and then stopped. And her eyes filled with tears. "I don't remember you," she said. "I was too little. But I knew your name."

She stepped closer.

"Good people took me in. Hid me. They said my father, Vasyl, had died in the first months of the war and my mother Ana, had died in the camp. And Halyna died soon after. We had to leave the village as they burnt the church and the town."

There was a pause—heavy, reverent—as if even the air had gone still.

"But I always felt like something was missing. Like someone was waiting for me."

Ana took her daughter's face into her hands.

"All this time…" Ana said. "I thought God took you from me."

Roza nodded, sobbing now, "But He didn't. He just… kept us apart. Until now."

The time stopped, then started moving back and forth as in a cuckoo clock.

What followed is easy to imagine: emotions flooding, tears falling, stories shared of the lives lived and lost, faith questioned and renewed. Paths once darkened by unimaginable pain now shone faintly with the light of miracles and hope. God's mysterious ways had woven two families together by the thread of a heart—a bond stronger than loss itself.

Silence. And then—

"But I knew," Roza said. "Somewhere inside me, I knew my mother was alive."

Ana collapsed forward, folding into her daughter. Wrinkled hands touched her wrinkled face. Roza was crying now, too, both of them shaking, rocking like a boat returning to the harbour.

Abi looked up at Ruslan.

"That's my…?" he began.

"Yes," Ruslan whispered. "Your aunt. Or… something like that."

"Baba's daughter," Abi said, blinking. "She's not lost anymore."

"No," Ruslan said softly. "She's come home."

The room blurred with tears and laughter, the wild sound of healing. Roza touched Abi's face. "This is the boy?" she asked Ana.

"My boy," Ana said. "And yours, now."

Roza nodded slowly, tears catching on the edge of her scarf. "She was my granddaughter," she whispered. "The donor. My Masha. She had your eyes."

The silence that followed held the weight of a century. Suffering had circled this family like a hawk, again and again. And now, somehow, life had cracked through the stone.

Ana pulled Roza in and kissed her forehead, just above the scar.

"We lost so much," Ana said.

"We did," Roza replied.

"But we also gained."

They sat together, time floating like cloth. Stories were told. Halyna was remembered. David too. And Bella. And Eli. The past didn't disappear. It didn't have to. It sat with them like a guest who'd finally been named.

Later that night, in the quiet apartment, Abi sat on Ana's lap, looking out at the city lights.

"Are you okay?" he asked.

Ana kissed his temple."I am now."

He leaned into her. "Baba?"

"Yes, dyto?"

"Does this mean you're not alone anymore?"

She looked out the window for a long time.

"No," she said. "None of us are."

And for the first time in a very long time, Ana believed it. She held on to the thread tightly, her heart beating steady, her scars still there but no longer visible.

Chapter Seventy-Seven
Far, Far Away

Far, far away from Ana's arms, a baby girl was carried through smoke and hunger. Halyna pressed her close, whispering lullabies in a voice that cracked, until rumours grew teeth and eyes turned sharp. Then the priest's family took her in, the wife kissed her small scar, and called her blessed.

By spring of '42, a grave carried her name, though she was not in it. The church burned, the priest and his wife with it. Halyna lay buried nearby, beside a stone that mourned a child who still breathed.

Roza's life unfolded in another town, another world, in the USSR. She grew up in the arms of the people who called her daughter. She learned to cross herself, kneel before icons, and braid her hair like village girls did. The war was already a story by then, told in loud voices and gaps in photographs during the May 9th Victory Day celebrations. The orphans grew taller, the widows no longer ached for their lost husbands, the wounded healed outside, but the scars still bled inside. The country built itself from the ruins, as did Roza, without even knowing it. And in a small Russian town, her days unfolded—there she grew up, there she grew old.

Once, when Roza asked about the pale scar on her forehead, they told her only this: "Your parents were Ana and Vasyl. Brave people. You were loved as we were told."

Then silence again. She learned to make do with silence.

At sixteen, she laughed too loudly with a boy outside the factory gates. She married him soon after. And six months later, her daughter was born. He drank too much, sometimes struck her, but life was heavy for everyone, and she carried it as she carried water from the well: one hand, then the other, steady enough not to spill. A son came next, his hair dark like hers, his fists always clenched as if he were ready to fight the world.

The factory became her second home. Machines drummed a rhythm into her bones, her hands smelling of metal and soap. She traded shifts with neighbours, queued for bread, and mended clothes by lamplight. She danced in the square at holidays, her laughter fierce and quick. She loved her children in the ordinary way: by scolding, by feeding, and by tucking them into beds that were never quite warm enough.

Her husband died before forty, the drink taking him as swiftly as war might have. Roza did not crumble. She worked double shifts, then triple, always with her daughter's hand in hers, her son darting ahead through the streets. Years blurred. Seasons turned. Her daughter grew and gave her a granddaughter-Masha—with eyes that sparkled like summer water. Roza held the baby close, breathing in her tiny weight, not knowing that one day that child's heart would beat inside her brother's son (the brother who had died before she even knew about him), far away.

Her life was not remarkable. It was lived—a courtyard filled with voices, the clang of dishes, the scent of laundry stiff with cold. There were aches and bruises, laughter and songs. There was survival without remembering why she needed to survive.

She knew only her name. The scar. The words: "Ana. Vasyl. Halyna"

That was enough to make her feel she belonged once, long ago, even if she could not recall to whom. Far, far away,

Roza lived a life. Not broken. Not unworthy. Simply lived. Not the one Ana imagined for her, but still alive and happy. And it was enough.

Chapter Seventy-Eight
Hineni, I am here.

Ana stood in front of the sewing table, the late light slanting through the window like gold dust. Outside, the city pulsed in its quiet summer rhythm—sirens distant, children laughing down the block, a dog barking at a leaf.

Inside, time was still.

Abi was reading in his bedroom. Ruslan was in the kitchen boiling water the old—fashioned way, even though the electric kettle worked fine. He said nothing when she told him not to—just nodded and did it his way as if he needed the pause, the waiting.

She understood that now. In front of her lay a length of soft silk—pale like bone, like memory. She had pulled it from the old chest yesterday, tucked between patterns she thought she'd forgotten. There were no roses on this one yet. Just empty space.

Ana sat down slowly, her bones complaining in quiet ways. She threaded the needle with red—not crimson, not blood—red, just red—full and unapologetic. She began to stitch—not carefully, not for anyone else, just for herself.

The first petal took form, slightly crooked. She didn't fix it. The second curled over the first, blooming without apology. Her fingers, though slower now, remembered. The muscle memory of mourning. Of making.

She didn't look up when Ruslan stepped into the doorway. But she felt him.

"He's sleeping?" she asked softly.

He nodded. "Curled up like a cat."

She smiled, pulling the thread through again. Ruslan stepped closer and watched her hands. His eyes followed the rose as it bloomed, thread by thread.

"Is this… for her?" he asked.

Ana didn't answer right away.

"It's for all of them," she said finally. "For Roza.

For those who had to forget themselves to survive.

For the mothers who lied to save their children.

For the boys who flinched before the blow ever came.

For Malka and her daughters, who never bloomed.

For Vera, who became the healer.

For Tosya, who fed us and kept us whole.

For David, who gave me another life.

For Vasyl, who called me Fire Bird.

For Eli and Bella, for their bright love—and for Abi, my reason to live now.

For a life that was decades of doing.

For you."

He didn't speak. But something in his shoulders loosened.

Ana tied the last knot and held up the square of silk. The rose was rough. Uneven. Alive.

She reached into the drawer and pulled out a pair of old, heavy scissors—the kind her father could have used that never dulled, no matter how many layers they cut through.

And then, carefully, she cut it down the middle. Then—into even pieces.

Ruslan tensed. "Wait-"

But Ana kept going. The tears were clean, final, and liberating. She placed the pieces into a basket.

"Come with me," she said.

Together, they stepped onto the small balcony. The sky had turned the colour of apricots, and the wind was warm and soft. Below, the city shimmered like a memory.

She held it for a moment. Then, she released the basket and the pieces. The silk caught the breeze and danced—not like a fall, but a flight. A soft letting go—maybe petals, maybe snowflakes, maybe little butterflies. Memories kept and letting go of the pain.

Ruslan watched them disappear.

She turned to him.

"I couldn't save them," Ana said. "But I kept the thread, all the memories. And now…"

When she returned to the table, she gently touched the thread and whispered, "I choose to sew again. Not to mend. But to make. Not because I must—but because I want. Because I am here, still here. Hineni."

Epilogue

This is not a story about survival, nor is it about the tragedies that threaded through Ana's life. This is a story about the will to live—even through death, despair, and the absence of hope. Even when there is no reason, fairness, or answer to why bad things happen to good people.

Because they do. Because pain does not ask who you are. And the world does not measure what you've lost. Good things happen to good people. Bad things happen to good people. And just the same—good things happen to bad people, and bad things to them, too.

The universe doesn't weigh souls. It spins. It shatters. It repairs. It spins again.

We do not mourn the loss itself. We mourn how we were with the people we loved—who we became in their presence. But when they are gone, we remain.

Hineni, I am here.

But when someone chooses to stay, love anyway, thread kindness through the wreckage, sew a life not out of what was given, but out of what they kept choosing,-they enter the unhappening cycle of untamed love.

And how we choose to exist—that part is still ours. And the story is for them.

About the Author

Solovey (a pseudonym) was born and raised in a country that no longer exists—a place that still lives in memory long after its borders faded from maps. Writing under a family name carried across generations, Solovey also means nightingale—an unassuming bird known for singing through the darkness.

"The Threader" is a work of remembrance and reinvention, weaving together history, memory, and the threads of survival. Through stories stitched from silence, Solovey honours the voices of those who came before and those who remain.

Solovey's love for storytelling continues in the forthcoming thriller novel, "The Godmother."

Contact:

Made in the USA
Coppell, TX
03 February 2026

70718854R00163